SHADOWMANCY

BOOK THREE OF THE NIGHTPATH TRILOGY

M. S. Farzan

PRAISE FOR ENTROMANCY: BOOK ONE OF THE NIGHTPATH TRILOGY

"Entromancy is that rare gem you find among the all-too-common dross of self-published novels. Author M. S. Farzan takes a premise that is truly unique and imaginative . . . throws in a diverse cast of characters, all to deliver an urban fantasy thrill ride."

--San Francisco Book Review

"In this rousing...science fiction novel, it's a futuristic San Francisco and the element [c]eridium has emerged as a renewed source of mythical power and otherworldly strength. Ceridium's side-effects, however, unlock mutative genes in the population resulting in a secondary race called [a]urics who become threatening to the human population. Thankfully, vigilant cops like Eskander Aradowsi are defending the races and reinforcing the safety of each. The narrative is fast-paced...this is a promising...launching point for the planned series."

--The BookLife Prize in Fiction

"Entromancy has been an amazing journey...which I think I would like to take again

*in the next book of the Nightpath Trilogy. The
world building is out of this world no pun
intended. If you like a lot of action, fighting and
guns a blazing then you are going to fall in love
with this series."*

--The Avid Reader

*"ENTROMANCY has one of the coolest
speculative fiction worlds I've encountered in a
while. The mix of magic and technology is an
amazing blend that results in all kind of
badassery from the characters. Backdropped
against a sort of dystopian/Philip Marlow-ian
cityscape, it felt like an epic D&D slipstream
universe...I recommend this book for anyone who
wants to get lost in an awesome world and/or
anyone who grew up on table-top role-playing
games."*

--Kit 'N Kabookle

*"I love all the characters in the book...I love the
little hint of romance that floats in the plot while
everyone get shot at. I really couldn't put this
book down once it got started."*

--Emily Carrington

*"This book was a fun to read story that centered
on several important issues concerning diversity,
differences, and deeply-held fears. I read mostly
to be entertained, but I couldn't help but think
about some of problems in terms of today's*

political climate. An attention-grabbing tale of conspiracy, hatred, and misconceptions that was easy to read, fresh, and frightening, my reading time was well-spent with this book."
--Laurie's Paranormal Thoughts and Reviews

"I am in love with the worldbuilding on this one. Seriously, it's amazing. It's hard to write science fiction with fantasy races and have it make sense, but by jove, I have now seen it done...I'd recommend picking this up if you like a good mix of science fiction and fantasy."
--Where Landsquid Fear to Tread

"I enjoyed the story a great deal...The plot was tense and also topical, which was a great boon to the book. I liked the way that current events were used to see a new race and a new world order."
--Judge, 25th Annual Writer's Digest Self-Published Book Awards

"Very vivid...Very compelling...Very fresh and punchy"
--Judge, 5th Annual Writer's Digest Self-Published eBook Awards

PRAISE FOR ENTROMANCY: A CYBERPUNK FANTASY RPG

BOOKS BY M. S. FARZAN

Entromancy: Book One of the Nightpath Trilogy
Technomancy: Book Two of the Nightpath Trilogy
Shadowmancy: Book Three of the Nightpath Trilogy
Jinnspeak

GAMES BY M. S. FARZAN

Entromancy: A Cyberpunk Fantasy RPG
Entromancy: Hacker Battles
Not-So-Super Villains

For Annie
You inspire me to follow my dreams,
no matter how crazy they may seem

KEY LOCATIONS

AURICHOME – Squatting less than forty miles from San Francisco proper in what's known as the "North Bay," the nation of Aurichome was once a haven for all races, but has recently seen its borders closed under the despotic rule of Agrid the Destroyer.

COLUMBUS-FARROW – The carnivalesque atmosphere of the city's North Beach district is punctuated by booming music, kaleidoscopic three-dimensional digital ads ("digads"), and neon lights. If there's action to be had, it can undoubtedly be found here.

DOWNTOWN – San Francisco, being geographically contained within a forty-nine-square-mile peninsula, was one of the first global city centers to begin building vertically in earnest. The skyline is crowded to the point of being impenetrable to all but the midday sun, and the auric-majority undercity reaches half as deep into the earth as Downtown's tallest building.

EAST BAY – What the East Bay lacks in glamor, it more than makes up for in diversity. Industrial shipyards and towering skyscrapers can be found alongside luxury houses and underground ghettos, and there are rumors of

safehouses and saloons located in abandoned
subway train stations.

GOLDEN GATE BRIDGE – The iconic
suspension bridge lay dormant and decrepit for
a period of two decades, caught in the crossfire
between Aurichome to the north and the Pacific
South NIGHT headquarters. It has since been
returned to its former glory as a tremulous
show of peace between the two factions, serving
as an orange beacon spanning the San
Francisco Bay.

NEW CASTRO – Rivaled only by Columbus-
Farrow in its ostentation, the centrally located
New Castro is home to nightclubs, digad-pocked
virtual reality emporiums, and vacation suites.
It's sleek, it's sexy, and it represents the
absolute best that San Francisco money can
buy.

PACIFIC SOUTH NIGHT HEADQUARTERS –
Poised forebodingly on the island of Alcatraz in
the center of the San Francisco Bay, the three
ivory towers of the Pacific South NIGHT
headquarters house over two hundred NIGHT
agents, Inquisitors, foot soldiers, staff, and
officials. It has enough space for fifty virtual
penitentiary inhabitants, and is comparable in
size to the Pacific North NIGHT headquarters in
Seattle, Central West NIGHT headquarters in

Denver, and Atlantic North NIGHT headquarters in New York.

PRESIDIO – Once a military base, then a park, now an overgrown forest that abuts the Golden Gate Bridge to the north, the Presidio is a not-so-mute testament to the societal and magical issues that plague modern societies. Filled with ragers and worse, the Presidio has been reported to feature a naturally occurring source of ceridium, although no faction has yet been publicly willing to send its forces to investigate.

RICHMOND-SUNSET DISTRICT – Ordinary people have to find somewhere to live, and in San Francisco, the Richmond-Sunset District is their best option. Soaring apartment buildings, underground housing structures, and the ever-present dual layer of traffic all dot the landscape, along with a visibly Aurichome-themed sports bar known as *They Might Be Giant.*

SANTA CLARA – Having boomed and busted multiple times over, Silicon Valley has continued to expand, finding Santa Clara to be its current hub forty-five miles south of San Francisco. All manner of technology - from drones and antigravity cars to cerujet engines and ceridium weaponry - can be found here, provided that one has the appropriate connections and pay grade.

SPARKS, NV – Two hundred and twenty miles to the east of San Francisco, beyond a dwarven outpost and the forgotten - but still neon - city of Reno, sits the tiny city of Sparks, Nevada. From this suburb appeared an augur known as the Sigil, who once took up residence in an open-air casino amphitheater in Reno, surrounded by drones and all types of machinery.

KEY PERSONAE

AGRID THE DESTROYER – A low auric entromancer known equally as "the Destroyer" and "the Betrayer," Agrid has the command of a legion of assassins that are loyal to his word alone, and is the new leader of Aurichome after seizing the throne by force with the help of the Unaligned in the Three Factions War.

ALINA "THE PITCHER" HADZIC – Former relief pitcher and owner of a revolutionary-friendly tavern in the Richmond-Sunset District known as *They Might Be Giant*, Alina Hadzic is a veteran high auric terramancer and Aurichome's former official Consul for Human-Auric Relations.

ANDREW ALYAWARRE – An Australian human auromancer, Andrew Alyawarre was coerced by the Unaligned to kidnap Aurichome's crown prince, allying himself with the auric nation after their help in recovering his sister, Celine.

CELINE ALYAWARRE – A teenage human chronomancer, Celine Alyawarre was abducted by the Unaligned during the events leading up to the Three Factions War and has since been traveling with her brother, Andrew.

DAMARA DRIVAS – (location unknown)
Cunning, driven, and deadly, Damara Drivas is
a human Inquisitor and formerly NIGHT's most
politically influential, public-facing figure next
to the Inquisitor General Marguerite Liu.

ESKANDER ARADOWSI – (location unknown)
Once spymaster to the king, Eskander Aradowsi
holds the dubious honor of being one of the first
high auric NIGHT agents, having made the
jump to Aurichome after a mission gone south.

FAZGHA HEZDOTTR – Queen of Aurichome,
Fazgha Hezdottr is a low auric terramancer and
the auric nation's leader in exile after King
Thog'run's disappearance during the Three
Factions War.

GLORIC VUNDERFEL – Gloric Vunderfel is a
gnome technomancer extraordinaire and
Aurichome's former Chief of Technology, having
recently taken over as the Sigil of Sparks.

KWAME DAIGAN – Kwame Daigan is a high
auric shadowmancer and friend to
Zzethromandus.

MARGUERITE LIU – Former attaché to William
D. Karthax, Marguerite "Madge" Liu is a human
Daypath of some repute and voted to be the
next Inquisitor General after her predecessor

abdicated the position under accusations of treason.

THE SIGIL OF SPARKS – Although the artificial intelligence experiment has failed many times over, rumors once boasted of a sentient, preternaturally clairvoyant leader who, just as strangely, took the form of an early-twentieth century automatic vacuum cleaner and was attended only by his cantankerous - and very human - Scribe. The charade of the augur's true form was exposed during the Three Factions War, resulting in Gloric Vunderfel taking over as the new Sigil.

STRIKER JOHNSON – Striker Johnson is a NIGHT agent celebrated for his efforts during the Karthax affair, although his metal arm, breastplate, and assortment of cybernetics indicate the toll the incident has taken on the human Nightpath.

THOG'RUN II – (location unknown) A low auric war hero and first sovereign of Aurichome, King Thog'run II is known far and wide for his battle prowess, tactical acumen, and brutal dealings with enemies of the throne.

TRIBE ACHEBE – A high auric vanguard and the adoptive nephew of King Thog'run, Tribe

Achebe is more often found causing problems for Aurichome than solving them.

VASSHKA "DOUBLESHOT" LESTRAGE – Known by most only by her moniker, "Doubleshot," the dwarf Vasshka Lestrage is a revolutionary in service to the crown and one of King Thog'run's former personal tactical advisors.

WILLIAM D. KARTHAX – A war hero and the former Inquisitor General of NIGHT, William D. Karthax was indicted in absentia for collusion against NIGHT while attempting to manipulate King Thog'run and Aurichome. Karthax has since been voted as the Mayor of San Francisco after allying with the Unaligned and promoting a xenophobic message against the auric-majority undercity.

ZZETHROMANDUS – Zzethromandus is an ancient shadow dragon and friend to Kwame Daigan.

PROLOGUE

It has been six months since what is being called the Three Factions War.

The following is my first log as the new Sigil of Sparks.

The previous Sigil was destroyed in a battle with Agrid the Destroyer, a low auric entromancer in the service of the Unaligned. The former, who is brother to Fazgha Hezdottr, queen of Aurichome and leader of the underrace nation, employed technomancers to raise lifeless dragons from beneath the earth, fusing them with machinery to create leviathans from the abyss. The latter have proven to be a devastating adversary for Aurichome and the National Intelligence Guard of Human Technology, known by most as NIGHT.

Originally conceived as a paramilitary force to contain the new races of people that began appearing in the early to mid-twenty-first century, NIGHT now serves as an armed buffer between humans and aurics, with their Pacific South headquarters located on the island of Alcatraz in the San Francisco Bay. A stone's throw away in the North Bay lies the underrace nation of Aurichome, NIGHT's bitter rivals and once led by the low auric warrior, Thog'run II.

I am complicit in King Thog'run's demise, by virtue of my inability to stop the Destroyer and the plot carried out by his factors in the Unaligned.

The Unaligned, or at least a splinter group thereof, overtook the previous Sigil by force, hijacking his massive network to pave the path for a coup within the ranks of both Aurichome and NIGHT. Numbered among them are assassins, mages, and of course, the technodragons that roam as nightmares throughout the Bay Area sky, impervious to the weaponry of the other two factions. Even the United States military, occupied as they are in protracted battles overseas, have proven ineffectual against the clandestine might of the Unaligned, who have claimed San Francisco as their own.

The new faction gained support quickly, and secretly, under the noses of NIGHT and my previous master, King Thog'run of Aurichome. Bringing the xenophobic William D. Karthax, the former Inquisitor General of NIGHT, into their fold, they spread an anti-underrace message throughout the Bay Area, initiating a revolt in the undercity below San Francisco just as Agrid brought his technodragons to bear in the forests above Aurichome.

The result, and ensuing fallout, has been catastrophic. Both the king and his Chief of Intelligence Eskander Aradowsi were lost in battle, their bodies as yet unfound. The throne has passed to Queen Fazgha in exile, as Agrid has assumed control of Aurichome with full authority. The current Inquisitor General,

Marguerite Liu, still oversees the NIGHT headquarters, but is powerless against the new leadership of Aurichome and the independent city of San Francisco, which designated a resurgent Karthax as its mayor in the recent public election.

Seeing the havoc caused by the decades of turmoil between NIGHT and Aurichome, thousands of humans have flocked to the standard of the Unaligned, joined by underraces who are afraid of the repercussions of dissent. A silent majority elected Karthax into power, making the Unaligned's rulership of the region complete.

The former Inquisitor General has begun building his barrier around the undercity, claiming that doing so will keep San Franciscans safe from the perceived threat of the underraces that have lived among them for over fifty years. I have helped to provide sanctuary for the queen, her loyal subjects, and others who are still true to the Aurichome of old, but I dare not reveal their location in this log. The previous Sigil proved to be many times the technomancer that I am, and yet he met his demise at the hands of the Unaligned.

I, Gloric Vunderfel, former Chief of Technology to the king of Aurichome, write not with hope that this log will be read, as it is encrypted within the same network that I have worked to rebuild after the Unaligned wrested it free from my predecessor. I write for the same reason as those that have come before me: to document the shifts of power that are evident through magic and technology, to read the patterns of human and auric civilizations and employ my network to promote balance among them.

I write, secondarily, for a reason that I suspect has been shared by the long line of Sigils that precede me, from well before the synthetic element of ceridium was discovered and revealed the genetic mutations that gave rise to the phenotypic variation of the underraces and the resource to power enchantments and spells.

I write because it is lonely to know everything, and to be bound by oath to share it with no one.

-The Sigil of Sparks

ONE

*"They have slept for a millennium. I do not
imagine they will be thrilled to be roused."*
          -Kwame Daigan, Master of Shadow

Contrary to all of my previous thoughts on the
matter, the future turned out to be eerily
similar to the present.

For six months, we walked the blasted land
above Aurichome, moths to a flame that
threated to overwhelm us on a daily basis. We
found safety among the gnarled trees that
ringed the giant clearing that was once a
battlefield, still recovering from the ravages of
magical war and time. Informants once loyal to
the throne met us at way stations, providing us
with food and news from within the undercity
beneath San Francisco, painstakingly putting
together piece after puzzle piece that had taken
decades to uncover.

It had taken me two weeks to emerge from
my time-warped daze, and another two to
comprehend the depth of the mess into which I
had been dropped.

My last memory of the old world was

shadowstepping to the back of a monstrous, magic-powered technodragon, only to be blasted by the foul breath of another of the beasts that had Agrid the Destroyer as its commander. I had been ensorcelled by a spell cast by Celine Alyawarre, a teenage girl who was just coming into understanding her chronomancy power, and fell through time and space to appear in a dystopian future, roughly thirty years ahead of my present.

Celine's spell had saved me, and ruined everything else in the process.

I had emerged not far from the battle site, in a desolate clearing where Agrid's technodragons had blasted the earth decades before. A much older and more powerful Celine had greeted me, along with an ancient shadowmancer named Kwame Daigan and a gigantic black dragon, Zzethromandus, who was an odd traveling companion. They took me into their protection, gently explaining the events of the past as I recovered from the mental and physical disorientation of being transported into the future, while keeping us safe from an enemy that always seemed to prowl at the corners of our vision.

Our nomadic lifestyle was difficult with a cerujet-sized dragon in tow, but not impossible. As a shadow dragon, Zzethromandus could cloak himself in gloom with a thought, obscuring him from all but the most discerning instruments at night. He spent most of the day away from the Bay Area, hunting or doing whatever it is that dragons do in their free time, communicating with Kwame by some unseen method to discern our location and join us after the sun had set for the day.

The shadowmancer himself was one of the most peculiar aurics I have met. He was extremely eccentric, preferring a thick, colorfully patterned Tibetan wool coat and simple breeches instead of more modern clothing, and had a deep, melodious voice that was accentuated by his archaic manner of speech. His skin had a translucent ebony hue to it, and as a full high auric, his ears were twice as long as mine, pierced with simple studs made from black pearl. I placed his accent from somewhere in West Africa, and in my six months of knowing him, he had proven to be friendly, if somewhat serious.

Celine, my other traveling companion, was just as strange, but in a different manner entirely. The aboriginal human moved with a preternatural grace that was almost otherworldly, and wholly unlike the young girl that I had met thirty years prior. She had mastered the nascent chronomancy ability that I had observed, and the potency of it followed her, sometimes trailing in her wake or flashing in her eyes when she was angry. Her broad features and curly brown hair had matured and softened with age, and although she retained the hearing disability from her youth, she often seemed to know what I was about to say before the words had left my mouth.

The events that had led me to appear in a not-so-distant, dystopian future were, at least as I understood them, a tangled mess that Celine, Kwame, and, less patiently, Zzethromandus had attempted to unravel for me on multiple occasions. As they would describe it, concurrent to my demise in the battle that had delivered me out of time, King Thog'run II of Aurichome had also disappeared, and the tide swung in the favor of the Unaligned, who had also initiated a revolution in the underrace-majority undercity below San Francisco. As NIGHT attempted to contain the fires that had been unleashed on the undercity, Aurichome and the Unaligned waged a terrible battle in the North Bay while four of Agrid's technodragons destroyed everything they came across. A terrible toll was paid as Aurichome's innards were laid bare by the unnatural beasts' magical breath, tearing through the bedrock to expose a terrified underrace nation underneath.

The Three Factions War lasted less than a week, as the aurikar survivors quickly capitulated to Agrid in the absence of their king, and the underraces living among and beneath San Francisco were cowed by the Unaligned, even with whatever meager protection NIGHT was able to provide. In a matter of months, William D. Karthax, my former boss in the predominantly human organization, was elected mayor, and the Unaligned's takeover of the region was complete.

The decades had not been kind to the aurics and humans of the San Francisco Bay Area. After ten years of haphazard authoritarian rule, Agrid had proven to be a terrifying dictator and a terrible administrator, running Aurichome figuratively into the ground as its inhabitants fled for dubiously safer pastures. The aurikar nation, once on the rise to greatness under Thog'run II and his family, was eventually abandoned, and my companions and I stalked the forests above a ruined city that was haunted with unachieved splendor. The San Francisco aboveground had become an unincorporated city and a bastion of humanity, with a wall built around the underrace undercity that made travel between them next to impossible.

To my knowledge, Karthax still lived, innervated by his Inquisitor magic or some foul mancy, and had suspiciously been voted in as mayor in every succeeding election, the irony of which was not lost on the company that I kept. After the crumbling and eventual abandonment of Aurichome, Agrid had disappeared, his technodragons lazily prowling the skies about Northern California, listless and riderless but no less dangerous to the cities below.

I hoped the low auric entromancer was rotting somewhere in a grave of his own making, but my instincts knew better.

Celine, with help from Kwame and Zzethromandus, had explained that she had met the latter two about ten years ago, after having returned to her native Australia in search of asylum. Her older brother, an auromancer giant named Andrew, had been killed in defending my friend and the new Sigil of Sparks, Gloric Vunderfel, and the young girl had no place to turn other than the home of her birth. Over time, she had come to terms with her magical prowess and became a chronomancer of no small repute, using her abilities to perform minor miracles in places of auric resistance around the world.

I wasn't sure how long Kwame had been walking the earth, but from the high auric's aged features and archaic speech, I guessed that he had been around for centuries. Unbeknownst to the general populace, he and Zzethromandus were the missing connection between the auric present and what Kwame called the "orichite" past, linking cultural histories of magic and fancy to a very real, and very dark, future. Their presence confirmed that the synthetic element ceridium, developed in the twenty-twenties by green researchers as a sustainable fuel source, once existed, centuries ago, in a natural form known as blue orichalcum. Then as now, the element powered magical spells collectively known as "mancy," and revealed a dormant mutation in some humans that, when exposed to ceridium or blue orichalcum, resulted in the phenotypic variation exhibited by the underraces, including low and high aurics, dwarves, gnomes, and trolls.

I have written elsewhere about the second-class citizen status of the underraces as they began appearing in the twenty-first century, but suffice it to say that their condition has been the complete opposite of their ancestors' counterparts. As Kwame describes it, in times prior to the western Dark Ages, aurics – then known as orichites – enjoyed their own civilizations that were coveted by the barbaric humans that prowled near their borders, calling them "elves," "orcs," and using other fantastic terminology to describe them.

Over time, humans became savvy to their neighbors' use of blue orichalcum, utilizing the element to power their own growing schools of magical knowledge and eventually exhausting the world's natural reserves of it. Within a century, orichites all but disappeared from the face of the earth, their features fading into obscurity as their genetic mutation returned to dormancy and they intermingled with human communities. The study of mancy lay barren as well without an element to power it, and magic became relegated to myth and legend instead of the factual history it warranted.

A small order of shadowmancers, numbering a solitary chronomancer among them, foretold of the depletion of blue orichalcum and subsequent decline of the orichites. They were treated with derision as misanthropes and forgotten when their divination had come to pass. The prophecy, outrageous as it may have seemed at the time, was that humankind would overtake the natural order, sending orichite civilization into darkness for an eternity, until a new source of blue orichalcum was discovered. The shadowmancers believed in the eventual resurgence of an orichite people, although the mechanism by which they would rediscover the element that is now called ceridium was unknown to them.

The shadowmancers, referring to themselves ridiculously as the "Masters of Shadow," sought to preserve orichite civilization by channeling their power into one being, safeguarding the essence of their magic within a vessel that was powerful enough to sustain it until the return of blue orichalcum. They made a deal with a dragon that was known to them, to use its body as the vessel and to instruct them in the intricacies of the shadow magic needed to enact the ritual. The dragon would disperse its power among three others of its ilk, awaiting a time foretold among them when blue orichalcum would resurface.

That dragon was Zzethromandus.

The Masters of Shadow spent a fortnight, years before the disappearance of blue orichalcum and the orichites from the earth, casting a long and winding spell that channeled their essence into Zzethromandus, who was to then disperse it among the three others of his kind. A shadowmancer was bound to him as a guide among humankind, should the dragon need one, and bereft of his power but still retaining his orichite form due to his connection with Zzethromandus.

The initial transformation of power was successful, but once the Masters of Shadow were gone, their power depleted and their bodies empty husks, the dragon was unable to complete the final spell to preserve the other dragons. Painfully, the beast sat and watched as his ministrations only partially took effect, placing the dragons in a kind of stasis that persisted until the present time.

Whether Kwame was the dragon's original guide, or has inherited the position from another of the Masters of Shadow, the dark auric hasn't said, but he truly has no magical affinity, shadowmancy or otherwise. His living curse has been to wander the world in search of a shadowmancer fit to complete the ritual and restore life to the other dragons, bringing the prophecy disclosed by the Masters of Shadow to culmination.

That, Celine revealed to me one night as we were discussing strategy after months on the move, was where I came in.

"You want me to what?" I had asked, trying to sort out my new companions' explanation of why they had brought me to a future dystopia and what my role would be in the weeks to come.

"We need a shadowmancer of some ability," Celine patiently explained for what must have been the hundredth time, "to complete the spell that the Masters of Shadow began, and bring Zzethromandus' kin back to life."

I swallowed, hard. I had been given extensive shadowmancy training in my time with NIGHT and was an adequate spellcaster, but sincerely doubted I had the aptitude to wake a sleeping gerbil from its slumber with my magic, let alone a dragon.

"I don't understand," I said, stalling, "There are plenty of NIGHT agents and others that are proficient with shadowmancy. Why not go to them?"

Celine shook her head gently, her long, gold earrings sparkling against her brown skin in the light of our little campfire. "None of the agents are of auric blood, which is a requirement of the spell."

That at least made sense to me, as my grandmother had the high auric gene, and passed it on to my father and his children. "Why wait until now, then?" I pressed. "Why bring me all the way to this wasteland instead of tapping me before the Three Factions War?"

Kwame cleared his throat, shaking a handful of sunflower seeds in his hand before popping one into his mouth. "I have been searching for a very long time, Eskander. First, we-" he waved a swarthy hand vaguely at the forest, as if to include Zzethromandus, who was roaming somewhere in the night, "-waited for centuries for blue orichalcum – what you call ceridium – to be rediscovered. Then we waited until the old ways were renewed, and mancy came to a suitable level of development.

"But we tarried overlong. It wasn't until several years after the Destroyer made his move against Aurichome that we met Celine, who remembered your sacrifice in the battle that began the Three Factions War, and vouched for your ability and orichite heritage."

"Wait," I protested, my head spinning. "Am I dead in this world?"

Celine shook her head again. "Not anymore."

"I was dead?"

"You weren't alive," Kwame explained.

"You'll have to be more specific."

"After I met Kwame, and then Zzethromandus," Celine took over, "it became apparent that the only way to undo what happened in the past, was to return to it. But deciding on a thing and doing it are two separate tasks entirely.

"It took me several years," she continued, "just to perfect the spell that would bring you here, and another six months for us to locate the sizeable amount of ceridium required to cast it."

I nodded dumbly. "How did you do it?"

Celine beamed, and for the faintest instant, I saw in her face a shadow of the girl I had helped save from the Unaligned's clutches years ago in the monster-overrun Presidio. "You'll recall that I cast a spell of quickening upon you on that fateful day," she said, recounting our battle with

Agrid's technodragons and the Unaligned. "That incantation provided a window in time with which to work, and the beast's foul breath was the catalyst in your time to help propel you to ours."

I remembered all too well the technodragon, clad in rotting flesh and metal machinery, spouting a beam of magic from its maw that was intercepted by Celine's chronomancy spell. "So the technodragon's breath sent me into the future?"

"Not exactly," Celine said, her voice still thick from the hearing impairment she had experienced since birth, but no less clear or powerful. "Time is not a fixed variable, as most people think; it is more of a river that ebbs and flows, rushing ever forward. If one knows how to swim against the current, one can manipulate their place in its passage.

"But even the most skilled chronomancer requires a power source to work against the natural tide. On our side of the river, we used a great amount of ceridium to bring you here. In your time, the beast's breath provided the fuel, while my spell indicated the exact location in which to find you."

My thoughts began racing again. "So I *didn't* die when the technodragon hit me with its breath?"

"You didn't," Celine confirmed, bringing the conversation full circle. "But neither did you live. You were transported to our time, without anything in between."

I sat back for a while, staring at nothing while Celine waited patiently and Kwame spit sunflower shells into the fire. I wrestled with the idea of asking about those close to me, of Alina, of my family and friends. I decided that I didn't want to know how they had fared.

"What do we need to do?" I asked after a long while.

Kwame smiled, his teeth white and a little predatory. "We need to wake up the dragon's family."

The plan, as it was explained to me, was to travel to the three locations of Zzethromandus' kin, awakening them from their stasis by channeling a shadowmancy ritual that Kwame, himself being bereft of magical ability, would teach me. Celine would then transport us back in time to do battle with Agrid and his abominations and, hoping against hope, forestall the apocalyptic future to which my companions had transported me.

It didn't sound easy, and the logistics proved to be even more complicated. For both the shadowmancy spell and Celine's attempt to return us to my time, we would need unusually large amounts of ceridium, which were ordinarily available only through official government channels that were not accessible to us as fugitives. Celine's factors had a lead on a potential source that was being stockpiled in the undercity below San Francisco, which was ringed on all sides by a now-ancient barricade that Karthax's people had constructed.

The scheme also presupposed that I had the magical prowess to bring dragons to life, about which I was skeptical. I resolved to take it one step at a time, having already spent months attempting to become accustomed to the idea that I had been transported in time and would have to learn some arcane shadowmancy spell for a shot at returning things to normal.

I slowly stood in front of the fire, latching my nightblade to its holster on my hip and stretching my back, which was sore from sitting.

"When do we get started?" I asked.

TWO

"Time is, quite literally, of the essence."
>   -Gloric Vunderfel, the Sigil of Sparks

It proved to be even more difficult than expected to break into the undercity.

After several days of meticulous planning, a lot of which was spent on catching me up to the current San Franciscan political climate, we set off in a southwesterly direction with the intention of approaching the city from the coast.

Although it had been thirty-odd years since Karthax rose to power as mayor of San Francisco, a loophole in the free city's legislation meant that he had somehow been re-elected consistently by a widening majority. The xenophobic sentiment within the metropolis had snowballed after the Three Factions War, driving the remaining auric minority back underground or fleeing to neighboring cities that supported more inclusive citizenship policies. Aurichome was no longer a safe haven for the underraces, ruled by an erratic and ill-equipped sovereign in the form of Agrid, eventually crumbling into dust after years of mismanagement and autocracy.

Karthax himself, from the augmented reality recaps that Celine had shown me, seemed to be a shade of the man for whom I had once worked, with none of the scruples. Time, and to my mind, a renunciation of values, had allowed him to lose his athletic, military bearing, and he now eschewed his customary fatigues for the suit-and-tie habit that was the hallmark of western politicians. His skin had taken on a ruddy complexion, with his blond-dyed hair swooping hastily from one side of his head to the other. Few reports discussed whether he retained his mancy skill as a former Inquisitor General, but at least some magically-derived vigor was apparent in his demeanor, even at his age of eighty-something. When he spoke, it was with hate, sometimes in direct reference to the underraces beneath the city, and other times in more elusive terms about outsiders encroaching upon San Francisco.

One of Karthax's first tasks in taking control of the city was to extricate it from the political clutches of those loyal to the old Aurichome, which went hand-and-hand with building a barrier around and above the undercity to prevent easy passage between the auric barrens and San Francisco proper. Checkpoints were installed in prominent locations such as Downtown, Columbus-Farrow, New Castro, and the Richmond District, with Karthax's own burgeoning militia handling the specifics of managing them, and not with a gentle hand. They were armed to the teeth with commandeered weaponry, given the colloquial title of "redhats" due to the security helmets they wore emblazoned with Karthax's standard.

Their methods and brutality made the general populace – the underraces among them – long for the days of NIGHT surveillance in its comparative tranquility.

Over the decades, the rules of passage between San Francisco and the undercity became more stringent, and the underraces that were either unable to flee, or had chosen not to, began to develop their own society in earnest belowground. They rallied around a leader, called simply the "Duc," who was unknown to the human population outside of the undercity, and apparently ruthless in his tactics in the ongoing fight with the world above. Auric assassins would appear without warning in San Francisco, committing acts of violence against the redhats, only to melt into the shadows before being caught by Karthax's people. Any attempts to invade the undercity openly or surreptitiously were rebuffed absolutely, with the Duc taking an extremely hard line against potential infiltrators in his midst. The Unaligned had pulled such a trick during my time, to devastating effect.

One chess piece in the underraces' possession was that they had gained control of the monster-ridden Presidio, which had long been locked away because of its dangerous denizens and erratic magical phenomena. No aboveground human dared come within its twenty-foot tall, long abandoned electric fences. From even before San Francisco became subjected to the control of Karthax and his redhats, there was rumored to be a naturally-occurring source of ceridium somewhere in the Presidio. As Celine and Kwame would tell it, the

Duc had been using it to help fuel the aurics' acts of guerilla warfare against the redhats, while also utilizing it for more mundane purposes like powering the undercity's technology.

To enact our dubious plan, we would need access to that ceridium – what Kwame and Zzethromandus called "blue orichalcum" – both to power my shadowmancy ritual and for Celine to send us back in time to do battle with Agrid and his technodragons. We would also need a spike in power to take place in the past to provide a doorway for us to appear, similar to the way Celine's chronomancy and the technodragon's breath weapon had brought me to the future. For that, none of my companions had yet proposed a solution, but one couldn't solve everything at the same time, I supposed.

From what I had heard of his dealings and demeanor, it was unlikely that the Duc would just hand over the blue orichalcum with a smile and a blessing. He was loath to work with outsiders, even aurics, and had snubbed all previous attempts at correspondence from Celine and Kwame. We would have to break through redhat security and traverse the undercity covertly in an attempt to parlay with the Duc directly, none of which sounded painless to me.

Our best bet would be to approach San Francisco from its west side, circumventing the redhat checkpoints by attempting to enter the undercity through a storm drain on the coast of Land's End that abutted the Presidio. It was unguarded by the redhats because of its proximity to the dangerous Presidio, and used sparingly by a group of underrace smugglers that were sympathetic to Celine's cause. They would meet us at the entrance and help usher us into the undercity, but after that, we would be on our own.

We started out at dusk, leaving the questionable haven of the ruins above Aurichome for the very tip of the Point Reyes National Seashore to the west. Celine's factors had provided us with a state-of-the art vehicle they called a "glider," which was one of the strangest modes of transportation I have seen. Technology had advanced quite a bit in the intervening thirty years, and antigravity machinery had become so ubiquitous that tire-and-chassis cars had become artifacts of the past. Gliders had replaced all but the most recent AG-boostered vehicles, and they provided for a strange and unsettling experience.

Our four-person glider was an oblong disc about nine feet long at its apex, with aerodynamic lines and a matte finish that made it look like a spaceship. Its tiny ceridium engine hardly made a sound, and it had a slanted glass casing that protruded from its top side to provide for a kind of cab for us to sit in.

I was grateful that Celine at least knew how to operate the vehicle, as it didn't respond to any sort of digitab, which, apparently, had also become something of a relic. Ceridium technology had developed to the point where one could have a ceruchip installed under the skin, and it would reference their thoughts and gestures to do things like control vehicles, access the network, and complete other tasks that people in my time would have used a digitab to perform.

We traveled, eerily silently, over dilapidated dirt roads that now served as animal trails in the forgotten environs around Aurichome. The inside of the glider smelled alien and sterile, and I longed to open a window to expose the cab to fresh Pacific air, but was unsure if the thing actually had windows and if so, how to operate them. Now and then, I would catch a glimpse of Zzethromandus' cross-shaped form between a break in the clouds above us, the dragon tracking our progress from a distance while avoiding any errant technodragons patrolling the heights.

The wind threatened to buffet the glider as Celine rounded a bend along the Point and, terrifyingly, took us straight over the rumbling waters of the coast. My stomach lurched as our quick turn forced the glider into an almost 90-degree rotation on its axis, before righting itself and speeding southwards towards the city.

The weather outside was as dismal as my queasiness inside the cramped vehicle. We sped over the churning waves past Point Reyes and into the Gulf of the Farallones, where a squall pelted us with fat raindrops that sounded like bullets against the glider's exterior. Celine hadn't said a word since we had gotten into the vehicle, concentrating on who-knows-what to make the thing move, and Kwame stared at the roiling waters outside enigmatically with his chin in his wrinkling hand. I was happy for the silence, afraid that were I forced to talk, I might instead expel the contents of my stomach.

The glider, which proved to be exceptionally fast, took us past the western side of the San

Francisco Bay in no time. The storm clouds obscured the Golden Gate Bridge and all but the brightest of lights from the city skyline from our view, and I had the distinct feeling of floating through a wet, foggy dreamscape into an unknown civilization that was anything but inviting.

I bit the inside of my cheek, hard, as the glider suddenly lurched to a stop, the rocky coast beneath Land's End on the northwestern side of the city appearing through the rain without warning. Celine, still concentrating but looking unconcerned, hovered us closer to the gravelly terrain, which glistened with rivulets of water that coursed towards the ocean.

The glider gently touched down on the rocks, lilting slightly as its landing mechanism found purchase on the wet soil beneath. The wet glass surrounding the cab fell away with a hiss, and I took a grateful, wobbly step onto a small boulder, being pelted by a torrent of rain for my trouble. Kwame, steady on the rocks as a mountain goat, signaled for me to follow him and Celine, indicating that Zzethromandus would circle above us in case we needed to make a hasty retreat.

Given my quarter high auric heritage, my vision was better than average, yet I could still see no farther than ten feet in front of me in the rain and darkness. There was no sign of people, redhats or otherwise, and the area around Land's End looked as though it had been utterly deserted for decades. Rainwater and sea spray bombarded the rocky coast, making our passage among the stones difficult and treacherous.

Just when I thought we must have taken a wrong turn, Kwame signaled for us to stop, his dark hands moving quickly as he fiddled with a pile of pebbles on the ground. He grabbed at something, motioning for Celine to help him, and the two of them exchanged words that were lost to the storm before they reached my ears.

Suddenly, the rocks next to them shifted, and what had appeared to be a barren expanse of vertical stone was revealed to be a large metal grate of antiquated design, rusted and green with mildew. I didn't know what kind of magic or technology had gone into the drain's concealment, but it was a good one.

Before I could think to caution him against doing so, Kwame stuck his head boldly through the grate, conversing with someone or something in the gloom beyond. A terrible stench of sewage or something worse wafted from the drain's opening, which was ten feet in diameter. A click sounded within, barely audible over the rain and ocean waves, and the grate swung open with a creak, Kwame dancing back to make room.

"Let us go," he said quietly, his eyes white in the darkness.

I followed the old auric and Celine dutifully, feeling out of my depth but grateful to be out of the rain. The grate swung closed behind us by an unseen mechanism, slamming with a muted clang that sounded to my ears of finality.
Kwame took us confidently deeper into the foul-smelling tunnel, and I scanned the walls for any sign of inhabitance.

If anyone had come this way recently, it didn't show. The storm drain was filthy, with a disgusting creek of sludge snailing inexorably towards the exit behind us. The percussive sound of dripping water served as a metronome, marking our passage with time. Once, as we moved quickly down the tunnel, I thought I saw a pair of eyes peering out from behind a crack in the wall, but our pace was such that I couldn't stop to investigate.

Celine had donned a simple woolen cap and bandana that covered her ears and face. It was unanimously decided that although she and Kwame had contacts within the undercity, her human features would be instantly recognizable among the wary aurics and might draw unwanted attention onto us. We had resolved that Kwame, who was a full high auric, would do the talking for us, and I would provide backup.

For the first time since being a NIGHT trainee, I was less than confident in my abilities to protect those around me. I still had my nightblade, and Celine had secured a peculiar, rod-shaped thing for me that was supposed to be an upgraded version of a ceridium pistol, but I knew very little about the dystopian version of an undercity that I had rarely visited even in my time. I was sure that the three of us could stand our ground against a handful of anti-human ruffians, but certainly not with an entire angry auric city on our tails.

The tunnel continued for half of a mile before spilling us out onto an old underground train track that ran perpendicular to our current direction. The track appeared no less abandoned than the storm drain but slightly less disgusting, with trash strewn about and a

different, more metallic stench. Kwame stopped
to listen at the opening, waving us to follow him
along the broader tunnel to the left.

I was utterly lost after fifteen minutes of
following the auric through the outskirts of the
undercity, over a handful of tracks and through
a series of tunnels and switchbacks that
exhibited no markings that I could discern.
Kwame walked with a surety that surprised me,
given that he maintained that he had never
stepped foot in the undercity, proclaiming that
Celine's contacts had shown him a rough map
and that he had an excellent sense of direction.

Over time, the tunnels gradually became less
littered with trash and more uniform, providing
us with the sense of a grid that had been laid
out in a similar fashion to the metropolis that
existed above. Maintenance shafts and train
tracks shifted into verifiable streets and
alleyways, with stout, hastily constructed
buildings that were either abandoned or
shuttered against the world at this late hour.

I jumped when we encountered a person for
the first time, a dirty-looking dwarf that was
hurrying past us in the direction from whence
we had come. I held my breath as he trundled
past us, looking wild-eyed and muttering to
himself, paying us no mind.

The undercity became progressively more
populated as we moved in what I thought must
have been an easterly direction. I had only
visited its outer environs as a NIGHT agent a
handful of times, thirty or more years before,
and everything about it felt foreign to me.
Startlingly bright neon signs began to dot our
surroundings, providing the only semblance of

familiarity to my time. They were attached by rickety hinges and cables to concrete domiciles that looked of dwarven make, stout and sturdy but bereft of adornment. The streets were narrow but provided enough space for one lane of traffic, and I saw a few parked vehicles that looked more akin to the AG-boostered cars of my day than the alien gliders of the future. Although time was meaningless this far underground, there weren't many aurics about at this time of night, and those that were seemed furtive and uninterested in our little group.

The whole scene reminded me of stories that I had read of countries like Cuba in the late twentieth and early twenty-first centuries. The San Francisco undercity was, to my eyes, like a time capsule, frozen in an epoch that had long passed and forced to utilize older technology because of politically driven tariffs and sanctions. The outsider's perception of the underraces as guerilla tacticians and terrorists was very real, due to their violent activity aboveground, but in the undercity, the aurics seemed to be just barely scraping out a livelihood.

My thoughts wandered to Thog'run II and his ascendancy to the throne of Aurichome. He and his aurikar refugees had likewise been called terrorists, and eked out an existence as they built a nation, although his citizens had fared quite a lot better under the low auric's authoritarian rule. I wondered what had happened to him during the Three Factions War, and if he had truly found his fate at the end of a technodragon's foul breath and claw.

A slight motion ahead of us drew me out of my reverie, and I cleared my throat to get Kwame's attention. The high auric's keen hearing picked up the sound, and he scanned the tight roadway, his shoulders tensing as he witnessed what I had seen.

Halfway up a tall, nondescript grey building ahead of us, the nozzle of a sniper's rifle tracked our movement, its owner hidden behind tattered purple curtains. That they hadn't picked us off indicated to me that they were watching our progress and not necessarily hostile, but I hated that we were completely exposed in the roadway.

My mind raced to think of escape routes in case things got ugly, as we were likely to blunder into trouble while attempting to run away from it. I had no way of knowing whether the sniper was simply protecting the neighborhood or had more nefarious plans in mind, and didn't want to draw undue attention upon ourselves by acting out of character.

For better or worse, my decision was made for me as we reached the end of our block. Eight aurics triangulated on our position, seeming to materialize from the concrete in front, behind, and to the sides of us with an assortment of weapons bared and threateningly displayed.

"These your people?" I dared to venture, speaking quietly and quickly to Celine as we halted, the aurics surrounding us.

She shook her head curtly, her eyes trained on the newcomers. They closed on us within moments, naked daggers, pistols, and shotguns gleaming menacingly in the neon light.

Unsure of the situation, I stayed my hand, waiting for Kwame to take the lead in case there was a way out that didn't involve violence. The high auric waited patiently, his eyes taking on a look of quiet resignation as his lips pinched into a thin line. Celine's posture, too, looked relaxed, her right hand casually brushing a satchel at her waist that I knew held her ceridium.

The gang's leader, a hulking low auric with two broken tusks that jutted out at angles from her leering face, strode to within striking distance of our group, a semi-automatic ceridium rifle strapped across her chest. She fingered the trigger threateningly as she approached, grinning maliciously.

"Money," she said without preamble, taking in our modestly kempt attire with a glance and clearly judging us as being out of place.

Kwame raised his hands placatingly. "We don't have any."

"Piss off," she said, or tried to, as she attempted to level the rifle at the ancient auric, murder in her eyes. Kwame shifted imperceptibly to the side, out of the line of fire, and dropped his forward palm in a downward chop, breaking the low auric's wrist while twisting the rifle out of her grasp with his free hand.

I didn't have time to consider the shadowmancer's blindingly fast speed as a dwarf to my left swung a wickedly curved shortsword at my midsection with a grunt. I slid back hurriedly, nearly tripping over a pile of trash at my feet. Overbalanced, the dwarf lunged forward, and I grabbed the sleeve of his thrusting arm, falling backwards and using his momentum to toss him over me and into the metal grill of a parked car.

He sailed over me to hit the vehicle with a crunch, falling to the ground in a heap. I jumped up into a ready position, ignoring whatever wet thing on the ground I had tumbled into.

A troll had advanced on Celine, swiping a crowbar at her covered head. It was a crude weapon, but huge, and wielded expertly by the auric, who was nearly one-and-a-half times the size of the small woman. To her credit, the chronomancer held her ground, staring calmly at the troll as she pinched a ceridium crystal in between her fingers and whispered words of power.

The spell took effect immediately, rendering the troll out of our time and into another. He froze in place, flickering, his arm outstretched and the metal crowbar shuddering to a stop mere inches from Celine's temple. The troll's broad, bearded face was contorted in a mixture of rage, surprise, and confusion, and he seemed to disappear and reappear in front of Celine at an alarmingly rapid rate.

As serene as Celine appeared in battle, Kwame was a bounding, twisting, and tumbling nightmare. Having made quick work of the low auric leader, he dodged out of the way of a ceridium shotgun blast to run up the weapon owner's thigh, wrapping his own quadriceps around the auric's neck and then lunging backwards to toss the offender, head-over-heels, into another encroaching gnome. The two aurics fell together in a heap, with Kwame landing lightly on his feet next to them after completing his backflip.

A low auric to my right leveled a pistol at me, steadying his aim on the hood of an ancient truck that had had its tires removed and squatted on crumbling grey bricks. I squirmed and ducked, feeling a ceridium bullet tear painfully through my left bicep. I hastily drew the ceridium wand that Celine had provided me, pressing a button on its chassis that activated its firing chamber. The thing *whooshed*, discharging a blast of blue light that arrowed towards the truck, scything through metal and leaving a trail of cobalt fire in its wake.

The low auric, surprised but unharmed because of my poor aim with the new weapon, sighted down his pistol for another shot, and then gurgled in pain and astonishment as a flash of blue sprouted from his throat. He slammed against the hood of the truck, which itself was smoking from my ceridium blast, and I followed the angle behind him to see the sniper's rifle still exposed from the building on the next block.

I turned to face the next combatant, but the remaining thugs were dispersing, having seen what our little group had done to protect ourselves and wanting no more to do with us. I sheathed my ceridium wand and clutched at the wound in my arm, gritting my teeth against the pain as I attempted to stem the flow of blood.

Noting my discomfort, Kwame picked his way among the bodies to help, tearing a piece of cloth from his woolen jacket and expertly fashioning a makeshift tourniquet around my bicep. He didn't seem to be breathing hard, even after his exertions.

Celine's eyes were fixated on the building ahead, searching for the sniper that had disappeared from its upper story window. The chronomancer waved a hand nonchalantly, releasing her spell on the troll, and the huge auric collapsed bodily to the ground, limp and unconscious.

The street was silent and still as a side door to the building opened soundlessly, and another troll sauntered out of it, a huge poleaxe in her grip and the sniper rifle strapped across her back. She was short for a troll, with dwarf-like horns protruding from her forehead, and a hodgepodge of metal and ceridium-reinforced armor fastened to her body.

Our group warily watched her approach. She had a regal bearing to her, her gaze strong and much less furtive than the few undercity denizens that we had encountered. She strode with confidence, the bottom of her poleaxe clicking lightly against the pavement with each step.

Celine put up a hand to stop the troll when she was just outside the reach of her poleaxe. "That's about close enough," the chronomancer said, her voice muffled slightly by the bandana across her face.

The troll glared at us, hard. "Newcomers," she remarked. It was a comment, rather than a question.

Kwame nodded, motioning to my bloody arm. "Our friend is hurt. Can you show us to a healer that can help him?"

Her eyes flicked to Kwame, then me, and

back to Celine. "The Duc sent me to look for you. Your people are very...persuasive."

If Celine was proud of her connections, she didn't show it. "We'd be glad to speak with him," she said smoothly.

Without further preamble, the troll turned on her heel, marching further into the undercity. "Come on, then," she said over her shoulder, and her voice had the tone of a military commander. "The Duc will be pleased to see you as well."

I found her confidence sincerely difficult to believe.

SIGIL'S LOG 1.2.140: THE ORICHITE AGE

Halyfax Dureaston stepped through the shimmering portal and appeared elsewhere. Whereas the sun had just been warming the tresses of her straight, strawberry blond hair, unfettered as they were from her heavy cowl, the rain in her new environs pelted her with dreadful force. The sudden change in climate still unsettled her, even after a century of teleporting across great distances.

The shadowmancer irritably pulled her cloak's black hood over her head, feeling it instantly dampen from the wetness that had already soaked her hair and long ears. Mud underneath sucked at her boots as she stamped away from her point of arrival, muttering to herself in a dead language in preparation for the impending summit.

The Arabs and Persians were still developing algebra as Halyfax sloshed through the swamp surrounding the island fortress. It was a world away from her haven of sun and seagulls, dreadfully miserable with its constant downpour and inclement weather. She knew from decades of experience that the summit's attendees were a distrustful sort, requiring outsiders to march the final half league on foot rather than allowing them to materialize comfortably within the stronghold's fortified walls. It still rankled with her that in this most propitious time of magical ascendancy, a person of her station should still be required to do something as mundane as walking.

They were right to be suspicious, she knew. The humans of Western Europe, even laboring as they were through the Middle Ages, had become keen on the use of blue orichalcum. Neighboring orichite kingdoms had become sympathetic to the relatively barbaric human enclaves, teaching them the ways of magic for some reason that Halyfax, herself a racial purist, couldn't fathom. The humans' application of mancy was brutish at best, and they were obsessed with destructive spells that gave them an advantage over their adversaries, rather than other, more sophisticated forms of sorcery.

The trend was similar in other heavily inhabited areas of the world. From smaller, nomadic tribes to stationary communities tied together by empire, the humans were absorbing orichite knowledge like sponges, for which Halyfax gave them a grudging if rueful respect. Magic had been on the rise for the past millennium, and if reports were to be believed, the earth's natural resources of blue orichalcum were in decline. Halyfax didn't share the same alarmist view of some of her fellows, that reserves of the magical element were nearing a perilous low and that their depletion would threaten the orichites' very way of life. Still, the humans' encroachment on their lands and sputtering, if mounting, control of magic gave her pause.

She trudged ruefully through the muck, the stormy weather matching her foul mood. The barbarians called her people "elves," "orcs," and other bastardized terms that their inelegant tongues twisted from their original pronunciations. They understood little about the true laws of mancy and even less about orichite civilization, but if their population growth continued, they would indeed threaten her people's borders in a matter of centuries.

The shadowmancer pushed the thoughts away from her mind as she reached the edge of the swamp, wiping the dampness from her angular face and with it, any sign of her brooding discontentment.

It wouldn't do to provide an indication of her resentful sentiment in the dispute that was about to ensue.

THREE

"Violence is the only language the redhats understand. We'll speak to them in words they can comprehend."

-The Duc of the Undercity

The troll took us on a winding route through the undercity, following enough alleys and side streets that my tenuous grasp of the undercity's layout was unraveled within minutes.

She introduced herself as Belinda Hernandez, one of the Duc's lieutenants and a former military officer. The sniper rifle on her back was old but evidently functional from our firefight, and her poleaxe was of a construction I hadn't seen, with a ceridium core glowing faintly in the dim street light.

Despite Kwame's ministrations, I had lost a good deal of blood, and the undercity swept past me in a blur as we made our way to the Duc's palace. The troll led us to an old fashioned, dark-windowed, ground-hugging van that I was grateful to climb into, and I registered none of the towering apartment buildings that scraped the cavern's ceiling overhead, nor the squat, neon-laced storefronts that lined our path. The undercity was still asleep as we drove between districts, moving from the trash-lined outskirts to what felt like a modest metropolis buried beneath San Francisco.

We were to not look to the Duc in the face, Belinda explained, as doing so would be perceived as a threat by the iron-fisted leader of the undercity, and to only speak when spoken to. I offered no protest, instead half-listening to the troll's conversation with my companions as Celine and Kwame plied her for information about politics in the undercity and their relation to the world above.

After an eternity of driving, peppered by a handful of coded exchanges between our guide and the Duc's agents, who waved us deeper into the undercity as they saw Belinda's van, we arrived at an unadorned granite building that was sandwiched between two similarly nondescript shops. The neighborhood was visibly more affluent than what we had seen, with cleaner roads and functional, if still ancient, vehicles parked along the curb. Still, the few passersby that we encountered were no less furtive than the ones in the undercity outskirts.

Belinda parked her van in an empty spot, scanning the roadway for watchers before exiting the vehicle and beckoning for us to follow. The troll strode up to the sandstone building, then crossed to the storefront to its left and waved a digitab at a pair of glass doors that hissed open as she approached. I found her method of ingress peculiar and familiar, given her usage of an outdated tablet instead of a subdermal chip like Celine's, but supposed it was yet another sign of the undercity's forced utilization of antiquated technology to go about their business. Celine and Kwame followed her warily, and I brought up the rear, clutching my torn arm and hoping that we would reach our destination before I collapsed. The troll led us through what appeared to be an antique weapons shop, dark and empty at this hour but somehow still feeling as though it was being surveilled.

Our march came to a halt as Belinda reached a wall on the right side of the store that featured an AR projection of assorted ceridium weaponry digads. She tapped the tip of her poleaxe against the wall, rattling a string of nonsensical words that must have been a code of some sort.

The wall shifted almost immediately, swinging away from us and into the granite building that we had seen from the outside. The sniper ushered us through the hidden door and into a spacious interior that was damp and echoey, smelling of mold and algae. Recessed lamps overhead provided a meager, soft light into what looked like a large parlor, with wide granite steps that led off to our left.

Auric guards, looking as edgy and battle-hardened as Belinda, watched our approach, glaring at the sight of newcomers. I attempted to return a particularly surly-looking dwarf's glower with a sweet smile of my own, but the pain from my arm turned the expression into a grimace.

No one questioned our passage in the presence of the sniper as she walked confidently up the steps and over a small stone bridge that traversed a rushing underground river, which, even in my hazy mind, registered as being somewhere underneath the Mission of San Francisco as it had been an age before. I took a mental note of our location in case it became useful at a later time.

At the top of the steps was a small veranda that overlooked the river and would have been pleasant if it were less austere. The spartan terrace hosted a dozen or so rough-looking aurics who scowled warily as we approached, and two long tables that projected augmented reality holograms of aboveground San Francisco with strategic markers placed at specific locations.

It was a war room of sorts, bustling with tactical analysis even at this late hour. At its head across from us sat a slouched, tired-looking high auric with dreadlocks that were woven into a scruffy, brown-and-white beard.

I was careful keep my gaze away from the auric's face, recalling Belinda's admonition even in my depleted state. The troll stood at attention in front of us, partially blocking my view, and waited with downcast eyes until the Duc was ready for her report.

"Speak," he said at length, and in a gravelly voice that sounded oddly familiar to me through the pain.

Belinda cleared her throat demurely, but didn't appear to be nervous in the presence of her superior. "I've brought the chronomancer that the scouts reported. They encountered some trouble in the outskirts, and her friend is injured."

There was some movement at the head of the room, and a gnome detached himself from the Duc's side, walking over to me and passing Belinda as she continued her report. The gnome reached into dirty-looking robes and pulled out a glowing blue stone, crushing it in his palm as he gingerly took my arm in his free hand, chanting an incantation that I recognized from my time as a Nightpath. A photomancy spell, once reserved for Daypaths in the service of NIGHT, took effect, soft light filtering around my bicep and closing the wound instantaneously. I raised my eyebrows, wondering at how the regulations of magic had evidently become more porous since my time, yet still there were too few shadowmancers who could take my place in our mission.

I thanked the gnome, who nodded gruffly, and returned my attention to the conversation, which had become heated.

"We don't have it, and we wouldn't give it to you even if we had," the Duc was saying to Celine, his voice raspy and threatening.

The chronomancer, who had removed her facial disguise to speak honestly, boldly pressed her case, keeping her eyes fixed to the floor in front of the Duc's black, buckled boots. "Allow me to at least explain our intended use for the blue orichalcum before you make your decision. We need the element to power a ritual, that will create a gate in time for my companions to return-"

"I told you, we don't have it," the Duc interrupted Celine impatiently. "We barely have enough to keep the undercity running, let alone to power some useless chronomancy spell."

I felt Kwame's eyes on me, and looked to see him jerk his head towards the Duc, suggesting that I put a word in. I demurred, making a face to let him know that I doubted my luck would be better than Celine's.

"Then allow us at least passage into the Presidio, where we can retrieve it ourselves," Celine pleaded.

The Duc laughed, his voice echoing across the sandstone walls. "Good luck with that." He waved a hand, dismissing us, and Belinda turned to escort us away from the veranda.

As she did, Kwame stepped to the side, surreptitiously placing his knee behind mine and tapping a pressure point in my back that sent me skittering forward. I reached out instinctively, grabbing one of the long tables to steady myself before spilling ignominiously in front of the Duc and his people.

"What the hell!" I exclaimed, glancing back at Kwame in astonishment.

The auric guards gripped their weapons in reaction to the motion, tense. I stared daggers at Kwame, who again wagged his eyebrows pointedly at the Duc.

I followed his gaze up the Duc's seated form to his scraggly, bearded face and olive complexion, to dark, brooding eyes that were old and tired, and that I recognized.

"Eskander?" the Duc asked, looking at me quizzically.

"Tribe?" I guffawed.

"What the hell?" he said, echoing my earlier exclamation.

He was thirty years older, and more world-weary and battle-hardened than the upstart vanguard that I had once known, but there was no denying that the high auric sitting in front of me was Tribe Achebe, King Thog'run's adoptive nephew.

I looked back at Celine accusingly. "Why didn't you tell me that Tribe was the Duc?"

"I didn't know!" she protested.

"Leave us," the Duc commanded, and his guards filtered out of the room, save Belinda, who affixed me with a sidelong glance.

"Aradowsi?" she asked, trying to decipher the puzzle of my presence in her time. "You were supposed to be dead."

"You *were* dead," Tribe corrected, springing from his seat after the room had emptied. He strode in between the tables to stand, incredulous, in front of our group. "We all saw the holovids of you disintegrating in a technodragon blast during the Three Factions War."

I shrugged. "There's a lot to share."

We spent several hours exchanging stories, Celine and Kwame taking the lead explaining my travel through time and their plan to reawaken Zzethromandus' kin. Tribe described the demise of Aurichome under Agrid's reign and the subsequent eradication or exile of the royal family. Most of those loyal to the aurikar throne dispersed to the winds or were killed by the redhats, but Tribe, who was a thief first and a prince second, went back to what he knew best: surviving in the shadows. He made a name for himself as a smuggler in the besieged undercity, eventually rising to power as its self-proclaimed Duc and utilizing the same kind of guerilla tactics that made his adoptive uncle, the erstwhile King of Aurichome, infamous.

Uncharacteristically emotive, the vanguard-turned-Duc clapped me on the back more than once, the crow's feet at the corners of his eyes crinkling as he searched my face, remembering a time long past that for me had only been a matter of months. His touch and bearing displayed a command that I would never had thought possible in the impish rogue that I had first met at an illegal Oxidium dispensary.

The years had not been kind to him, or to anyone, it seemed, but as the Duc, Tribe had proven to be a capable commander and revolutionary fighter, protecting the undercity from the redhats above and securing enough blue orichalcum from the dangerous Presidio for his auric subjects to continue to exist. The element was raw, and not refined in the same way as its synthetic counterpart in ceridium, but it served the same purpose in powering spells and devices for those who knew how to harness its potency.

"How did you come across the blue orichalcum?" Celine asked at one point in our discussion, genuinely curious.

The Duc's eyes sparkled, a shadow of the mirth that was once his hallmark. "It found us," he explained. "Even before Karthax finished putting a wall around us, we had heard about a naturally-occurring source of ceridium within the Presidio.

"NIGHT knew about it," he continued, glancing at me, "and were investigating it when Karthax threw them out of the city. The monsters roaming the Presidio seem to be drawn to it, and the undercity aurics before my time came across it by accident when hunting them down. When I became the Duc, I had my people create a pipeline to bring it in, refine it, and use it for our own purposes so that we didn't have to depend on the outside world for anything."

I nodded, following his logic. "What is it, exactly?"

Tribe shook his head, any semblance of humor quickly drained from his face. "I'm still not sure, even after all these years. It's a mine of some sort, surrounded by the NIGHT facility that was built around it. The blue orichalcum we were getting from it is about a hundred times more efficient than ceridium, so we don't need all that much of it to power the undercity."

"'Were?'" Kwame asked, hearing the nuance in the choice of words Tribe used to describe the source. "Do you no longer have access to it?"

The Duc shook his shaggy head solemnly. "It has become too dangerous," he explained. "We have an access point to the Presidio in the undercity near the source, but I've lost too many aurikar to make it worth our while. We have enough blue orichalcum to last another year at least."

I chuckled, having some idea where this would lead. "Point us at it," I said with confidence. "We have a dragon."

Tribe matched my flippant remark with seriousness. "Can your dragon destroy a chimera's nest?"

"A what?"

"There are a lot more monsters than when you last visited the Presidio," Celine interjected, referring to when I had helped extract her from the clutches of the Unaligned in the build up to the Three Factions War.

I nodded knowingly. "Ragers and other, less natural beasts."

"More of the latter, and a lot of them," Tribe said, which gave me pause. From well before my time, the Presidio had been inhabited by aurics that exhibited the rage plague, an illness of unknown origin that could only be mollified by use of an addictive chemical known as Oxidium. Oxidium, which had been introduced during the first generation of aurics as a potential "cure" for the underrace gene, had proven to be more trouble than its worth, equivalent to a narcotic with short-lived superhuman-enabling abilities.

"What kind of resistance are we looking at?" I asked cautiously.

The Duc walked to one of his tactical maps and waved his hand over it, bringing up an AR hologram of the Presidio. He spread his fingers, expanding a small area that outlined a crumbling, ramshackle building in the midst of trees.

"This is the old NIGHT facility," he said, pointing at the building, "about half a mile from our access point here in the undercity. A chimera and other monsters have taken up residence in the building, feasting on the blue orichalcum and claiming the territory as their own."

"You're not able to drill upwards to the mine from within the undercity?" Celine asked reasonably.

Belinda, who had been quiet, shook her head. "It's bedrock. We don't have the equipment."

"I don't see why Zzethromandus can't just destroy the building and everything inside of it," I complained, returning to my original suggestion.

Kwame looked doubtful. "If the chimera draws its power from blue orichalcum, I would hesitate to learn what it could do with a dragon's life force."

I grunted, conceding the point. "What about the ragers?"

"Very few, if any," Belinda said. "Since Neoxidium, there have been fewer and fewer cases of the rage plague."

I frowned, not understanding. "Neoxidium? A new version of the drug?"

Celine nodded. "After Oxidium was exposed as the driving force behind the rage plague, a new formulation was created that has the same restorative results, but without the negative side effects."

I felt myself rock back on my heels. "They found a cure for the rage plague? I thought Oxidium was the only stopgap against it."

Tribe looked at me with an expression that was akin to sympathy. "So did most of us, thirty years ago. Through advances by auric scientists, the rage plague catalyst was traced back to an unambiguously non-essential chemical compound within Oxidium. The whole thing unraveled after that, and the powers that be scapegoated the pharmaceutical conglomerate that initially introduced it as a salve against the auric mutation."

My mind reeled with the implications, and at the once flippant thief's nuanced analysis of the complex history. Thousands, if not tens of thousands, of aurics had devolved into fury-induced madness in my time because of the rage plague, without a cure or clear understanding of the origin of the disease. That it was intentionally introduced by an addictive drug that purported to make the underraces look more "human," while also being the only reliable remedy for rage plague symptoms, was truly heinous.

"Who knew about it?" I asked, my mouth dry.

"NIGHT, certainly," Tribe said without hesitation. "Maybe not at the outset, but for sure by the Three Factions War."

"Who introduced it, then?"

The Duc smiled sadly, his thoughts revisiting old and dark paths. "We think it was some precursor to the Unaligned, in the guise of pharmaceuticals. No one's taken direct responsibility after all this time."

"Someone who truly hates aurics, evidently," Kwame added.

I bit my lip, disbelieving. I was less surprised that NIGHT, a paramilitary organization that had once been synonymous with my professional identity, knew about the nefarious origination of Oxidium, than the idea that a splinter group would be capable of concocting such a calamitous catalyst for the rage plague. It had been a pox upon underrace communities since they had begun appearing with the advent of ceridium, and its origin proved to be more reprehensible than I had understood.

"How do we deal with the chimera, then?" I asked, tearing my thoughts away from the ragers.

"The old fashioned way," Tribe said, pointedly moving aside the folds of his jacket to reveal the worn leather armor beneath and dual daggers at his hips. It seemed that the old vanguard had not shied away from getting his hands dirty in the thirty years since I had known him.

"Why not send your people in to retrieve the blue orichalcum, then?" Celine asked cautiously.

"It's too dangerous," Tribe repeated, "and we haven't had King Thog'run's Chief of Intelligence with us." He smirked at me, using my old title from Aurichome's height of power.

I gave him a dubious look, thinking that Celine and Kwame would prove to be more effective than I ever could be in a time that was not my own, and to which I was still becoming accustomed. From the way they carried themselves, both Tribe and Belinda appeared to be stronger assets than a timesick Nightpath, as well.

"Come on," the Duc continued, clapping me heartily on the back. "It'll be like old times. And fun!"

FOUR

"Mancy is more nuanced than most aurics and humans realize. One cannot simply say a few arcane words, toss a ceridium capsule in the air, and create a cataclysm. Unless one is a dragon, whereupon the ceridium is not necessary."

-Kwame Daigan, Master of Shadow

The Duc allowed us a brief but precious rest before we set out from his palace, traveling in Belinda's ancient van, its tinted windows hiding our identities from view.

I did my best to focus inward while Belinda drove us northwest through the undercity's one-way streets, concentrating on the teachings that Kwame had been attempting to impress upon me during the past few months. As a former Nightpath, I had been given formal shadowmancy training, but within my first few minutes of working with Kwame, it became apparent that my mancy skill was paltry compared to his vast knowledge and experience. Because of the ritual that bound him to Zzethromandus, he couldn't actually cast any spells, which sometimes made it difficult for me to reproduce his instructions, but I was a dutiful student, determined to learn what he had to offer and put it to good use.

I had already picked up a number of useful shadowmancy spells in our training, drawing upon my own experience to add the esoteric gestures and words to my repertoire. The intricacies for the ritual that would reawaken Zzethromandus' kin still eluded me, proving to be extremely complex and exhausting for someone as uninitiated as I was, but Kwame continued to be a capable and patient teacher that was undeterred by my slow progress.

Traveling by van, we reached the access point in less than an hour, shortly after what would be sunrise in the outside world by my estimation. Belinda parked in an empty lot in the midst of an industrial section of the undercity, pipes and wires crisscrossing among metal and concrete buildings that powered hundreds of homes and businesses.

There had been very little discussion of strategy, given that our approach would be a smash-and-grab, attempting to get past the chimera's nest and stock up on blue orichalcum as quickly as we could. Belinda carried a reinforced pack the size of a K-9 drone that could store the arcane substance, and we hoped to be in and out of there within a couple of hours.

A few early risers worked the ceridium power plant adjacent to our parking lot, giving us no more than a passing glance as they surveyed a broken capacitor hatch in their dirty blue and white jumpsuits. I smirked at the irony that because of Tribe's secretive nature and the stipulations around not looking him in the eye, there would be few if any undercity citizens that would recognize the Duc among the general populace. He could essentially move about anonymously, which I supposed suited his lifestyle well.

Belinda led us down an alleyway between the power plant and a foul-smelling sewage treatment center to a stone wall that appeared to be a natural feature of the undercity cavern. She waved her digitab in front of a simple digilock attached to a chain link fence that ran the length of the wall, and a gate within the fence unlatched with a click. The troll swung the gate outwards, sidling along the small space between the fence and stone to a vertical fissure in the wall, which had steel rungs worked into it and was cunningly hidden from view.

Surefooted, the sniper clambered up the rungs and out of sight, and the rest of us followed suit. I brought up the rear, my arm sore but functional, and I soon regretted our choice of ingress into the Presidio as the climb continued upwards to the bedrock ceiling of the undercity and beyond. I like to think of myself as being in good shape, yet my shoulders and quadriceps were burning before we even reached the midway point of the makeshift ladder, and my recently injured arm throbbed with the effort.

Belinda drove a merciless pace, and we eventually reached a hatch at the top of the fissure, requiring the troll to provide her digitab credentials again to open. Cautiously, the sniper released the hatch and popped out into the world above, allowing cool, damp air to spill into the crevice. I breathed deeply, trying to infuse my numb arms and legs with energy, and grateful for the fresh air that was a marvelous counterpoint to the staleness of the undercity.

I followed the others up out of the crevice, heaving myself over the lip of the hatch and gratefully spilling onto a patch of grass that was still wet from the night's rain. Belinda soundlessly closed the hatch behind me, and I looked around to get my bearings.

We were in a forest, deep within the Presidio, non-native pines and eucalyptus trees providing a cover for tangled underbrush that had thick, weed-strewn grass scattered among it. The defunct military base-turned-public space had been overgrown in my time, but in the future, it was nothing short of a jungle.

The area around us smelled fresh, but *felt* wrong. My quarter high auric genetic makeup was not as sensitive to the presence of magic as were most full bloods, but even I could sense a strangeness that pervaded the grove into which we had emerged.

Belinda crept confidently to the west, silently motioning for us to follow. We made our way in between the trees, our attempt at stealth made easier by the wet leaves underneath that wouldn't crunch when stepped on. Our single-file line consisted of Belinda, her sniper rifle gripped casually in her huge hands and the poleaxe strapped across her back, followed by Tribe, his wickedly curved twin daggers looking like an extension of his fists, Kwame, who was unarmed but still dangerous, Celine, whose hand hovered protectively near her pouch of ceridium, and then me. I was still hesitant to use the ceridium wand in my possession even after seeing what it could do, but neither did I want to be forced into my nightblade's close range with whatever fiends we might encounter. I tentatively drew the wand and pinched it awkwardly in between my thumb and forefinger, hoping I wouldn't set it off by accident.

The hairs on the back of my neck were standing up by the time we reached a small clearing, and I could see by Tribe and Kwame's alert postures that the high aurics were uncomfortable as well. The touch of power in the air was palpable, but there was a perversion in it, like honey over milk that had spoiled.

The setting was incongruously at odds with the sensation. Whereas the undercity was stale, and suffocating under hundreds of tons of rock, nature had reclaimed the Presidio, and the morning sun filtered through the leaves overhead to bathe the clearing in gold brilliance. A light breeze caressed my face with the scent of pine and cedar, and the rain had brought with it a dampness that was pleasant and invigorating.

The absence of sound, however, gave me pause. We hadn't seen any animals on our short trek, and I could hear no birds or squirrels in our immediate vicinity. I knew that whatever unnatural thing had taken up residence in the NIGHT facility was enough of an aberration that the surrounding wildlife knew to steer clear of it.

Belinda stopped at the edge of the clearing, signaling to indicate she would cover our advance with her rifle. Tribe took up the lead spot, crouching as he silently moved into the clearing, keeping his body low in the tall grass.

A large, crumbling building loomed in front of us, ugly and at odds with the encroaching nature. It appeared to have been hastily constructed and subsequently abandoned, with broken scaffolding still attached to one side of it and drooping from the rain. Patches of roofing were missing, exposing the interior of the building to the elements, and the wood and plaster that made up its walls were threadbare and pocked with rot.

If there was movement within, I couldn't see or hear it from our vantage, but the one-story building was long enough to house ten Merlin-class walker drones or five of Belinda's vans.

I gave a low, sharp whistle, drawing the attention of the group in front of me. Tribe, at the front, turned to see what was the matter, and I motioned him over to me.

"Whatever's in there," I said, having second thoughts about our plan, "it'll be certain death for us to just walk into its house and try to take over, particularly if it's using the blue orichalcum as a source of power."

"What do you suggest?" Celine asked quietly, crouching in the brush.

I drew a simple map in a patch of mud with a stick. "One of us goes in there and draws them out. Then Belinda and the rest of us can pick them off one-by-one as they exit the building."

Tribe shrugged. "Fine, I'll go."

I shook my head. "You're too important to the undercity. Let me do it."

It was the Duc's turn to resist. "I already watched you die once. I'm not doing it again."

"Allow me," Kwame offered. "They won't be able to catch me."

I nodded, believing him. Tribe looked doubtful, but at a nod from Celine, he waved his hand, acquiescing.

We crept to within twenty feet of the building, sliding almost to our bellies to remain hidden among the tall grass. The feeling of potency was undeniable at this distance, as was the sensation of wrongness. Kwame detached himself from our group, a shade against the brush, and slunk his way to the lip of the foundation that encircled the building, slithering onto the concrete and up against the wooden exterior.

I held my breath as he peeked in between a gap in the front wall, and aimed my wand at the entrance to the building, which was slightly ajar. Satisfied, Kwame sidled over to one of the facility's broken windows, peering through the dirty, jagged glass to survey the scene within.

He stared for longer than I would have liked, but his body posture remained relaxed, and he soon scampered back to our group, his dark eyes noncommittal.

"I can see the mine from the entrance, but not any movement," he said, sounding frustrated. "I can *feel* something, though."

I nodded, knowing what he meant. "Feel like going in?" I asked, not really wanting him to.

He shrugged. "Other suggestions?"

Not receiving any, he shook his head in resignation, and crawled back up to the front door. Easing it forward with one hand, his other fist tightened with anticipation, he poked his head into the building. The high auric's long ears twitched as he peered inside, and he glanced behind the open door before disappearing into the building.

Almost immediately, I saw something detach itself from the ceiling within and drop into the space where the shadowmancer had just been standing. It was amorphous, constantly shifting in form, and hideously disgusting. One moment it drooped like a slug, and the next, it was prickly and unevenly shaped, and it humped weirdly after Kwame, who had moved deeper into the building.

I gave a yelp to alert my comrades of the danger, instantly regretting my suggestion for Kwame to enter the facility alone. Running heedlessly after the thing, I pointed my ceridium wand at it, firing a bright ray of azure through the open doorway and into what I thought may be its flank.

"Don't!" Tribe cautioned alarmingly, but it was too late. The blast hit the creature with its full force, but instead of being harmed by it, the chimera seemed to shift its blob-like body around the ceridium and absorb it fully, spinning in a half-circle to face me. Without preamble, it dove through the entryway, leaping the distance between us to land in the grass in front of me and swipe at me with a makeshift appendage.

I yelled again, surprised, as it hit me with a claw, tearing a gash in my thigh. I rolled with the movement, trying to take some sting out of the blow, but still feeling my skin and muscle split painfully from the attack. The chimera was huge, and disturbing, with teeth and claws appearing here and there only to become reabsorbed in its blob-like body. Its movement defied reason, and the thing made no sound and gave off no smell, adding to its otherworldliness.

A ceridium bullet dissolved into its milky carapace as Belinda made the same mistake that I had, but before the chimera had a chance to retaliate, Kwame came bounding out of the building, jumping and shifting his body into a devastating flying side kick that knocked into one of the creature's shifting heads with a crunch. It reeled backwards as the shadowmancer landed in a roll, scuttling out of harm's way. It seemed that the chimera could be damaged with normal attacks, if not ceridium-empowered ones.

Before anyone else could move, the creature reached up into a cone-like shape, emitting what could only be called an inhuman howl, and things got undeniably worse. From the surrounding forest, a host of aberrations came to its call, growling and gnashing beasts that had become twisted by the chimera's foul magic.

A two-legged, humanoid wolf thing raced towards Tribe, but the vanguard was ready and waiting for it as it closed the distance in seconds. The wolf-man grasped at the high auric with long, fetid claws, and the vanguard ducked under its foul embrace, spinning as he dropped. One of the Duc's long daggers flashed in the sunlight, hamstringing the creature and hobbling it to one knee. In the same motion, Tribe completed his turn, slicing his other knife across its throat and spilling its purple lifeblood to the ground.

Simultaneously, a bat-like creature the size of a rotodrone dive bombed at Celine, who made a warding gesture with her forearm and pinched a ceridium crystal in between her fingertips. A rift in time appeared, and the evil little thing flew into nothingness and reappeared harmlessly behind the chronomancer, where it took a bullet from Belinda's sniper rifle and fell among the grass, lying still. Celine gave a little wave of appreciation to Belinda's post at the side of the clearing, and turned her gaze to the chimera, which was preparing for another attack.

Another wolf-thing demanded my attention, dashing awkwardly on its hind legs to snap at my face with its jaws. I smelled its putrid breath as I ducked out of the way, drawing my nightblade in my free hand and slicing it across the beast's chest in the same motion. My attack drew blood, but the creature advanced towards me, its forepaws slicing the air in between us.

I backed away, my injured leg buckling beneath me, and swiped the nightblade in front of me to create some distance. The wolf-thing appeared undeterred as my sword clanged off of its claws, and I threw myself backwards into the grass as it strained its powerful neck towards me for another bite. Instinctively, I fired the ceridium wand at its face, and the blast sheared the beast's head from its shoulders, disintegrating it. I managed to scoot out of the way as the aberration's body fell to the ground, twitching.

Meaty thuds continued to fill the air as Belinda's sniper rifle took out more of the bat creatures, while Tribe and Celine fended off the chimera's minions and Kwame attempted to occupy the monster's attention. The shadowmancer was like a gnat, peppering the chimera with strikes only to dance out of the way of its snapping jaws and clawing swipes, and I discerned that he was leading it away from the building, knowing that if it was able to return to its den, the monster would be able to feed from the blue orichalcum and regain its strength.

I pocketed my wand, drawing a ceridium capsule from my long coat and crushing it while reciting one of the spells that Kwame had taught me. A shadowy carbon copy of myself materialized beside me, mimicking my movements and providing an alternate target for the monsters.

I gripped my nightblade with both hands, hoping that although it was reinforced with a ceridium binding, the blade itself was of ordinary make and could potentially do harm to the chimera without being absorbed. Dashing towards the creature as quickly as my injured leg would allow, I timed my strike so that Kwame could backflip away from the thing after dealing another blow.

I caught the chimera by surprise, if such a thing was possible, and grunted with a diagonal downwards strike that sheared off one of its toothy heads. The appendage fell to the ground with a sickening splash, dissolving in blue goo. The chimera shifted its body towards me, caterpillaring in my direction with blinding speed, and clapped two claws together in an attempt to grapple and absorb me into its bulk. It caught my shadow double instead, destroying it with a pop and slashing at empty air.

I used the chimera's movement to shuffle to the side, springing forward again with a thrust from my nightblade. It breached the thing's shimmering husk wetly, driving to its core like a knife through gelatin. The chimera shuddered, jerking the sword from my grasp, and I moved away from another bite from one of its jaws.

Free for the moment, Tribe appeared behind the chimera, launching himself up in the air from the back of a downed beast. His eyes glinting gleefully, he brought his twin daggers down in front of him with the full force of his body, burying them into the chimera's milky carapace. The creature trembled again and swatted him away with a club-like tentacle, and the vanguard hit the side of the NIGHT facility heavily, falling to the concrete foundation in a heap.

Moving even more erratically than before, my nightblade sticking out of it like a toothpick, the chimera advanced on me, and I struggled to scuttle away from its grasp after having put more pressure on my injured leg. Kwame used the distraction to close the distance, jumping and turning to uncoil like a spring and backhand the creature with a powerful fist.

The chimera anticipated the blow, turning its attention away from me at the last second to catch Kwame's arm in one of its maws. The shadowmancer shouted in pain as the beast's teeth found flesh, tearing into his arm and shaking him like a rag doll.

I dove at the creature, grabbing the hilt of my sword and wobbling it up and down in an attempt to do damage or at least draw it away from Kwame. My attack worked a little too well, and the chimera rushed at me, swallowing the nightblade whole and covering me with its weird, shifting bulk. I felt my face and chest crush with its weight and immediately panicked, being suffocated by its form.

As quickly as the pressure began, it was released, the chimera's nebulous body wriggling off of me in a manner that suggested pain. Tribe's daggers were sticking out of it like antennae, and the vanguard had skipped away from its erratic trembling, looking battered and dismayed that the creature was still moving.

Without warning, another wolf-thing appeared in the air just above the squirming aberration, teleported through time by one of Celine's spells. It fell, mid-swipe, on top of the chimera, tearing out one of its throats but not before being impaled by a spike in its carapace. The two beasts convulsed in an unholy embrace before lying still, the chimera dissipating into flaccid jelly that stained the grass.

With a whoop, the remaining beasts fled the clearing, the chimera's unnatural hold on them released. I dragged myself to the wolf-thing, heaving its slimy body over to retrieve my nightblade, wiping it in the brush and offering Tribe his daggers. The vanguard received them gratefully, cleaning them in a fold of cloth from within his jacket. He looked bruised but relatively unharmed, and I turned to see how my other companions had fared.

Kwame appeared to be in the worst shape, his arm torn and drooping at his side, although his gritted jaw was the only sign of pain from the stoic shadowmancer. Celine had a nasty gash from a claw swipe across her cheek, and she was rummaging in her pack for something to apply to Kwame's wound.

Belinda trotted up, her footfalls heavy in the grass and her rifle strapped across her back next to the poleaxe. Concern was etched across her features as she took in Kwame's condition.

"Should I call in a healer?" she asked Tribe, as much for the rest of us as for the shadowmancer.

The Duc nodded his head, dreadlocks bobbing. "Should be safe now."

We waited, panting in the grass, as a handful of the Duc's guards made their way through the undercity and up to our location at Belinda's call. It was midday by the time the gnome photomancer – Harbrick, Tribe said his name was – made it to us and was able to tend to our wounds. By that time, my leg was numb and Kwame had turned an awful shade of grey, but Harbrick's magic proved to be potent, fueled as it was by the blue orichalcum. I would walk funny for a couple of days and Kwame wouldn't be able to use his arm for a week, but we'd live.

In front of his people, Tribe took on an authoritative air, and I was happy for him to direct traffic, instructing his guards to form a perimeter and extract as much blue orichalcum as possible in reinforced packs like the one that Belinda wore. With the chimera eliminated, the Duc was confident that they could return to the mine when needed, but with the Presidio being as dangerous as it had been, there was no telling when something worse might take up residence in the area.

I took a moment to peek into the building, curious as to what the mine looked like. I had once been in a ceridium development facility, impressed by the science that went into synthesizing and refining the element that powered a quarter of the world, and was still amazed that its counterpart, blue orichalcum, was at one time found organically in nature.

The interior of the defunct NIGHT building was trashed, with rotting floorboards and overturned furniture that were marred by scorch marks from previous battles with the chimera. It was filthy, and smelled of mildew, but at its center was a moldy wooden framework that looked like an archaeological dig site. The scaffolding looked like it wouldn't support a child's weight, let alone a group of miners, but it encircled a ten-foot-radius pit that extended far beyond eyesight into the bowels of the earth, somewhere adjacent to the cavernous undercity. Sparkling with a sultry, matte blue glow, crystals that ranged in shape from small pellets to fist-sized gems encrusted the stone walls of the quarry, infusing the air around them with a smoldering sapphire radiance.

It was beautiful, and raw, unlike the manicured potency of ceridium. I knew instinctively that the mine was the source of the power I had felt upon entering the clearing, now unmarred by the presence of the aberrant chimera.

Our packs full, we returned to the access point, which proved to be its own ordeal, given that I could barely use my leg, and Kwame's arm was out of commission. We made painstaking progress down the hidden cleft and back into the undercity, preferring to take

Belinda's tinted van back to the Duc's palace rather than riding, exposed, with his guards in their cruisers.

It had been a rough night, followed by a worse morning, but we had at least secured the blue orichalcum that Celine would need to enact the spell to send me, Zzethromandus, and several other dragons to the past. I was no closer to perfecting the shadowmancy ritual to reawaken Zzethromandus' kin, but hoped that Kwame's tutelage would prove effective in showing me the ropes in time.

I caught myself mid-thought, thinking of my friends in the past, of King Thog'run, of my family, of Alina. I forced my hope into determination, knowing that my only route back to them and towards a better future than the one I currently inhabited was through Kwame's ritual, and through my mastery of shadowmancy.

I had to succeed. There was no other choice.

SIGIL'S LOG 1.2.193: THE ORICHITE AGE

"I don't see what the drakes have to do with it," Rakk Monduur rumbled, slamming his fist down on the circular table. The low orichite's long, braided topknot quivered with his emphatic movement, and his curving tusks gleamed with spittle. "The realm of sands is well-protected from the humans, and they are of a nomadic sort, unwilling to encroach on our lands."

"The humans call it the 'Sahara,'" Fey Chazmir chided her compatriot, a pompous edge sharpening her sweet voice. The gnome wore an exasperated expression on her delicate features, clearly tired of the discussion that had begun to circle.

"It matters not what words they use, nor what they do," Intari Intuis countered, lending her voice to Rakk's argument. She was an elder among the group, her wiry brown hair turning grey at the roots and giving the troll a regal look about her. "They take our names for their cities, and twist our knowledge for their warfare. They are pests, nothing more."

Halyfax was careful to keep her face neutral as the other Masters of Shadow argued, weighing what was being said against her own reservations and allowing none of her thoughts to alter her disinterested expression. There were fourteen of them assembled, and the summit had been ongoing for hours, without a resolution. Yet, the canny shadowmancer knew that she would be able to alter the outcome with a few carefully placed comments.

At least the fortress interior was more pleasant than the torrential climate outside. Thick, cold raindrops, almost hail, pelted the stone walls, providing the heated discussion with a percussive backdrop. A huge hearth, magically lit, warmed the large meeting chamber, which was dusty from disuse. The Masters of Shadow met in summit sparingly, preferring to send missives by spell rather than teleporting from their respective domains around the globe to the fortress, far to the west of what would be known centuries later as the British Isles.

"We have not survived for centuries as we are by being incautious," Harald Stouthammer offered reasonably, to a chorus of agreement from several other attendees. The pragmatic dwarf folded his hairy hands on the wooden table in front of him, his thick black beard disappearing within his heavy robes.

Fey nodded at the dwarf's comment, her chubby cheeks red from the warmth in the room. "Even if the humans do not pose a real threat, it harms none of us to at least prepare for every possible eventuality. Kwame has walked among them, and among the shadow dragons as well. He knows better than we the course that we should set."

"Then he should be here to speak for himself," Yakra Yakasa, a powerfully built high auric, groused insistently. She gestured pointedly at the empty stone chair in their midst, receiving a murmur of support from a handful of the Masters. It was well known among them that Kwame often kept his own counsel, preferring to venture among the human and orichite civilizations himself rather than emulate the reclusive nature of the other Masters of Shadow.

Fey shrugged noncommittally. "His attendance to our summit, or absence from it, does not change what we all know to be true. The humans have become wise to our ways, and there simply is not enough blue orichalcum to sustain their growing populations."

"Bah!" Intari guffawed. "They have barely gained proficiency in the destructive arts, let alone the true intricacies of orichite magic."

"True as that may be," Harald conceded, patiently retreading ground that the summit had already discussed several times over, "they are an eager sort, and may threaten to overwhelm us if their use of the element continues in this manner."

Rakk was shaking his head with every word, the long topknot waving against the back of his chair. "What *may* happen is of no concern to us," he grunted gruffly. "Even if what you say comes to pass, it will only affect those orichites that have been foolish enough to keep their kingdoms within reach of the barbarians."

In their endlessly roundabout way, they were getting to the heart of the dispute. The Masters of Shadow had dedicated themselves to the study and practice of their art, which, for most of them and their devotees, engendered a solitary lifestyle away from orichite civilization. Kwame had proven to be the only one among them that actually seemed to *enjoy* walking among the orichites and their human neighbors, learning their ways.

"It harms none of us by being cautious," Harald repeated his earlier admonition.

"You clearly haven't spoken to Kwame about what he proposes," Intari said bitingly.

The troll's comment piqued Halyfax's interest, but she chose her words carefully, still unwilling to take sides.

"What exactly does he plan to do?" she asked smoothly.

"It's...a ritual of some sort," Harald said falteringly, himself not clear on the specifics.

Intari nodded, for the first time in agreement with the dwarf. "It is at that. I visited Kwame a fortnight ago, anticipating his absence at our summit. He described the ritual to me in detail."

The others, including Halyfax, sat up from their comfortable positions, listening in earnest. Only Rakk kept his composure, his dark eyes unreadable and tusks glinting in the magical firelight.

"What do you know, Intari?" Yakra asked, her strong features pinched as she queried the elder troll.

Intari leaned forward over the circular table, intent on making her case. "It is a long, complex ritual, requiring much planning, and even more blue orichalcum. Kwame has already spoken with several of the dragons about it, and they have agreed to train us in their own shadowmancy to execute the spell."

Halyfax's delicate eyebrows rose at that, both in curiosity and trepidation. It was rare for dragons and their ilk to share their knowledge, even among the most learned orichites, but a threatening undercurrent in Intari's tone gave her pause.

"It is complicated, and dangerous," the elder troll continued, certain that she had captivated the attention of the other summit members. She tapped a sharp fingernail against the wood beneath her hand, eliciting a shrill rasp that punctuated her statement. "And it will be our undoing."

FIVE

"Of all the schools of magic, entromancy is one of the few that still provide some modicum of mystery. I have pored over the logs of my predecessors for signs of its origination, but its mechanism of operation as yet eludes me."

-Gloric Vunderfel, the Sigil of Sparks

I'm not quite certain what I expected to happen once we had secured enough blue orichalcum to power Celine's spell, but the chronomancer's first words upon our return to the Duc's palace genuinely surprised me.

"Let's contact Gloric," she said without preamble after Tribe had dismissed his guards in the interest of privacy.

The vanguard's eyes lit up at the suggestion. "Vunderfel?" he exclaimed. "The Sigil? I thought the Destroyer got to him decades ago. Where's he been?"

I felt my heart leap into my throat with excitement as well. Had Gloric somehow survived Agrid's attack on the Sigil's sanctuary?

Recognizing our shared misunderstanding, Celine gently shook her head, patting the air soothingly. "Not the Gloric in our time," she clarified. "The one in Eskander's time."

My excitement plummeted into confusion. "Contact him how?" I furrowed my brow. "You want to bring him here, like me?"

The woman shook her head again, rummaging through a pack of the blue orichalcum that we had acquired and producing a fist-sized gem that was pulsing with rays of sapphire and cerulean. "By this time, young Celine will have made her way from Aurichome to the Sigil's sanctuary in Reno with Andrew," she explained, referring to her older brother and guardian. "I'll just need to make a connection with her as a conduit, and the Sigil's network will take care of the rest."

"How do you know where she'll be?" I asked, genuinely perplexed.

The chronomancer looked at me like I had three heads. "I was there, obviously."

Tribe came to my rescue, similarly confused. "I think he means to ask, how can you track where she'll be in the past if...it's in the past?"

Kwame stepped in, understanding our bewilderment. "When Celine brought Eskander through time," he explained, "a new timeline was created. Its beginning was marked by his appearance here in our time, and continues from there."

"What," I said, still confused.

"Your first day here, in the future, marks the same time as the past," Celine said, her back to me as she scraped lines in the floor with an edge of the crystal. I sometimes forgot that she had a hearing impediment as she seemed to be able to know when others were speaking without having to read their lips. "When we contact Gloric, it will have been several months hence in his time, as it has been in ours."

"So," I struggled to follow the logic. "When you send me back, it'll be months *after* the Three Factions War, when I disappeared?"

Celine looked back from her work with a winning smile that made her look thirty years younger. "Precisely!"

"OK," I said, although it was not.

The woman completed her design, a spiral etched in the stone floor of Tribe's war room, although the Duc seemed to be looking on with curiosity instead of irritation at the graffiti. Celine stood at the origin point of the spiral, holding the blue orichalcum between her palms, and began to cast.

A beautiful litany, wordless and transcendent, escaped from her lips, filling the sandstone room with sound and power. It reminded me vaguely of her brother's musical skill as an auromancer, but Celine's spell was tuneless, ebbing and flowing as if by whim but somehow mellifluous. The crystal within her hands began to spin on its own volition, spiraling in time with the chronomancer's song and dwindling in size as its magical energy fueled her spell. Simultaneously, the spiral in front of her throbbed with power, glowing with an ethereal luminosity that lit the war room with cold blue fire.

Celine let her open hands fall before her, the blue orichalcum whirling crazily in front of her and now no more than a pebble, its power nearly spent. The chronomancer's eyes snapped closed, her broad features pinched in concentration, and her voice trailed off abruptly as the spell completed and the crystal disappeared.

She opened her eyes, which shone with cobalt fire, and spoke as though from a great distance, her voice thrumming with a thousand timbres.

"Speak, Eskander. The Sigil can now hear you."

My earpiece buzzed suddenly, a line opened through Celine's magic in the future to the Sigil's technomancy-empowered network in the past. I cleared my throat, awkwardly put on the spot.

"Uh, hello?"

Gloric's piping voice greeted me from the other side of eternity. "Nightpath? Where are you?"

It warmed my heart mightily to hear the gnome, even calling me by a former title that I had repeatedly resisted. "Not *where*, Gloric," I said meaningfully. "*When.*"

It was the Sigil's turn to be confused. "What?"

I took several minutes to explain how Celine's spell had worked, the gnome confirming on his end that the younger version of the chronomancer was indeed in his presence and serving as a conduit for the magic. To his credit, the technomancer didn't seem to flinch at my explanation, grasping the inner workings of the magic faster than I had.

"I did not foresee this," he said simply.

"Tell me about it," I replied.

"The others will be happy to hear that you're alive. There was an extensive search for yourself and the king, to no avail. NIGHT held a memorial service for you as a former agent, and even included a procession for Thog'run, given that Aurichome is in turmoil. It was nice."

I hedged, not certain that I wanted my friends to know that I had survived, in case we weren't able to make it back to their time. "Can you keep this between us, Gloric?"

There was silence on the line as the Sigil considered my request. "I won't mention it," he said at last. "Now tell me about the future."

I continued to discuss history's course over the past thirty years with Gloric as the others set to work, using Tribe's strategic AR maps to iron out the details for the next phase of our plan. I had the distinct impression that the Sigil was taking notes, feeling a little bit like I was revealing winning lottery numbers to a bookie.

"So what do you plan to do?" Gloric asked, matter-of-factly, when I had finished bringing him up to speed. He hadn't seemed to mind that he had been killed by Agrid the Destroyer in the future.

"Kwame has been instructing me in a shadowmancy ritual that will reawaken Zzethromandus' dragons, and they're our best chance at overthrowing Agrid's technodragons."

"Why didn't they just do that in the past?" Gloric asked honestly.

I shook my head. "Kwame ran out of time. They needed to find a shadowmancer with auric blood, which has been difficult to come by because of NIGHT's stranglehold on shadowmancy training. It wasn't until Celine met me in the past, and then found Kwame in the future, that they were able to put all the pieces together."

"Hmm," he said over the line, thinking. "Which dragons are we talking about? And how are you going to get them back here?"

I ticked off each of the names and locations on my fingers, having memorized them from my conversations with Kwame and Zzethromandus. "Korrastuus, eastern Europe. Achivverrus, Central America. Hokkozeratus, sub-Saharan Africa. Celine is going to use the same spell that brought me here to send us back."

"That's going to take a hell of a lot of ceridium," Gloric said without hesitation.

I nodded. "We just retrieved a stash of blue orichalcum from the Presidio. It should be enough."

"There's blue orichalcum in the Presidio?" the Sigil sounded surprised.

"There is *now*!" I exclaimed. "I'm not sure about in your time."

"Sounds thin," Gloric replied, commenting on our plan. He was right, but we didn't have a better option at the moment.

"It is," I admitted. "And we need some help from your side of things." I explained that, similar to the way that Celine transported me to the future using the technodragon's breath weapon as a catalyst, we'd need a sizeable magical event in the past to provide a window in time for me to jump through.

"That's not how magic works," Gloric protested.

I pinched the bridge of my nose, frustrated with my lack of experience on the subject. "I'll put Celine on the line later and she can discuss the details with you. Can you create a technomancy rift in time or whatever?"

"I forgot how difficult you make things, Nightpath."

"I'll make it up to you," I promised, then thought of another snag in the plan. I looked over at Celine, who had left her station at the tip of the spiral to pore over a holographic map of Guatemala with Kwame. "How do we get in touch with Gloric when we're ready to begin the chronomancy spell?"

The Sigil answered before Celine got a chance to respond, his voice buzzing in my ear. "While you were incorrectly describing the spell, I set up a time-capsuled relay that will allow us to chat over the network. You should be able to reach me on this line."

My eyes went wide over the implications of Gloric's technomancy skill as the new Sigil. "Can you do that?" I asked incredulously.

"I can now, having read the signature of Celine's spell," he said without pride or arrogance. "Would you like to hear the technical details?"

I shook my head, impressed but not that interested. "You can tell me later."

Neither Gloric nor I were ones for exchanging pleasantries, but I couldn't deny feeling better for having spoken with someone from my own time, and a friend at that.

Tribe provided us with personal quarters in his palace, which were comfortable for the following week that we spent recuperating and planning, but it was an otherwise miserable stay. As a surface dweller, I was unfamiliar with spending long stretches underground, and the claustrophobia had become oppressive after our first twenty-four hours in the undercity. It wasn't exactly safe for our group of newcomers to explore the area around the Duc's palace without drawing attention to ourselves, so I spent most of my time in Tribe's war room, examining AR maps or watching the underground river wind its way through the stone, turning Kwame's teachings over and over in my mind.

The shadowmancy ritual was long, complex, and borne of a time when magic was even more commonplace than it was after the discovery of ceridium. It had somatic as well as verbal components, gestures and words that felt alien and ancient on my unpracticed hands and tongue. The spells enacted by the Masters of Shadow held only a passing familiarity to the shadowmancy that I had learned as a Nightpath, and I struggled to keep up with the archaic incantations.

It didn't help that although we still had a few weeks to complete the ritual and rouse the dragons, our timeline for returning to the past was not infinite. Given that time continued to progress in the past as we were experiencing it in the future, it had been several months since the Three Factions War when Gloric received my call through Celine's spell. As history would determine, hostile relations would escalate further between Aurichome, NIGHT and the Unaligned in a matter of months, and the cost would be irreversible if we weren't able to return in time.

I didn't relish the road forward. To resurrect Zzethromandus' dragons, we would have to journey to each of the locations that Kwame and Celine had identified, which would prove difficult as cerujet travel was out of the question. The heavily-regulated aerospace industry would require background checks and DNA scans for each of us, and we were all ghosts on the network. Our options were to either travel astride Zzethromandus' back across deserts and oceans to the locations of his resting kin, which sounded terrifying, or utilize the newly-recovered blue orichalcum to fuel Celine's chronomancy.

The woman was confident in her ability, in the presence of a powerful enough source and a detailed map of the terrain, to open time rifts that would deposit us close to the dragons. Each spell that she cast would require her to remain with the portal to keep it open and provide us with a route home, which would be taxing. She assured us that because she would be teleporting us within the present time and not into the past or future, doing so wouldn't require another source of power at our destination as it would for the final spell to return us to do battle with Agrid's technodragons.

We opted to give it a go with Celine's chronomancy, due in no small part because it sounded better than riding a cantankerous shadow dragon over thousands of miles of potentially hostile territory.

One other wrinkle was the time it would take for each of the dragons – provided that I could correctly revive them, with Kwame's help – to travel from their current locations of repose to our predetermined meeting place, the ruins above Aurichome. To accurately deliver us to the right time and place in the past – what Celine called a "window" – we'd need to be in the same location in the future, with bursts of power for us to ride at both ends. The blue orichalcum in our time and Gloric's technomancy in his would provide the magical route for us to follow, so to speak, and Celine's chronomancy spell would be the guide.

I hadn't given much thought to what we would do once returned to the past. The presence of four more dragons would undoubtedly be noticed instantly by the Unaligned. We would have to prepare for immediate battle with Agrid's technodragons, which were essentially technologically-enhanced abominations created from the resurrected corpses of magical beasts similar to the ones protected by the Masters of Shadow's ritual.

I pushed thoughts of the future, or more accurately, of the future past, from my mind, focusing on the present. A mountain still remained to be climbed, first by reawakening dragons that had slept for a millennium, and then by riding the waves of time from a dystopian future to a past that, to me, now seemed very far away indeed.

I found myself hoping anew that we were up to the task.

SIX

"History has a way of correcting itself. The injustices our people have faced at the hands of the Unaligned will be reconciled in time, but at their expense, not ours."

-The Duc of the Undercity

Kwame appeared at the door to my quarters a week after we had first visited Tribe in his palace.

"It's time," he said simply.

I looked at him with surprise and not a little resignation. "I'm not ready," I complained, having only just begun to grasp the shadowmancy ritual that would be required of me.

He nodded knowingly. "I know," he said. "But we have to get moving."

I couldn't argue with that. Our timeline was getting preciously thin, and the longer we stayed with the Duc, the more opportunity there was for us to draw attention to our presence from the redhats above.

We met the others in Tribe's war room, the Duc flanked by Belinda and Celine, discussing final preparations while poring over yet another map, this time of Aurichome.

Tribe looked up at our approach, sympathy in his brown eyes. "I'm sorry that I can't go with you," he began regretfully. "There is much to do here, and in the case that you're not able to-"

I waved away his concern. "I understand. Hopefully we'll see each other again in the past."

He gave me a curious look at that, as though he were considering the idea for the first time. "That's right," he said. "If you *do* succeed, all of this," he gestured to include the expanse of his palace and the undercity, "will cease to exist."

I looked at Celine, who gave a curt nod. It seemed harsh that we were attempting to erase thirty years of history to provide for a better future, but I had to remind myself that the time in which I had found myself was not my own. I had been ripped from my timeline to prevent this exact turn of events, and had to follow through with our chosen course of action to ensure that the Unaligned were not able to steer history down such a dystopian path.

"Belinda will join you," the Duc said, mastering whatever emotion he was experiencing upon contemplating his own annihilation. "You'll find her to be an asset as I have."

I raised an eyebrow. "Seriously?"

The troll shrugged, looking uncomfortable. "I suppose I don't have anything keeping me here," she said, her large green eyes skipping for a second to Tribe's shaggy face. In that instant, I recognized their deeper relationship, and how much they would be sacrificing to change the course of their own past.

"Will that create any problems in time?" I asked Celine honestly.

She looked at me blankly. "I'm a chronomancer, not an augur," she chided.

I shrugged, not certain of the outcome but desperate for any help that we could get. "Alright then."

We said our goodbyes, commissioning Belinda's tinted van to drive us through the undercity and west to the outskirts near Land's End. We carefully emerged through the storm sewer in the dead of night to find our glider, covered in dirt but untouched, and sped north in another unnerving, but gratefully less turbulent, trip up the coast.

The ruins had changed little during the time we had spent in the undercity, and Zzethromandus was waiting for us in the unnatural clearing where I had appeared several months before. Kwame and the dragon had some unspoken manner of communicating, and Zzethromandus was characteristically testy when we arrived.

"I grow impatient with the constant delays," the dragon said in his deep, multi-resonant voice as we clambered out of the glider.

"Holy," Belinda oathed as she first caught sight of Zzethromandus, a towering shadow against the trees and lit by a gibbous moon overhead. The dragon was sitting back on his haunches, his wings folded behind him with their clawed tips brushing the blasted earth beneath. His reptilian snout caught the moonlight, glimmering ethereally as he spoke, and his long horns curved backwards, giving the semblance of a crown on his triangular head.

"You get used to it," I offered, speaking both about Zzethromandus' intimidating size as well as his cantankerous disposition.

"Eskander is near to replicating the ritual," Kwame replied without apology to the grumpy dragon.

"Your words do not instill confidence, shadowmancer," Zzethromandus grumbled. I couldn't help but agree.

"We'll begin in the morning, after us lesser beings have had the opportunity to rest," Celine said, and not without sarcasm.

The dragon harrumphed, stretching like an enormous cat and using his powerful hind legs to spring into the air. He gave a brief and sudden beat from his broad, batlike wings, and was gone.

"He really is dramatic," I said to no one in particular.

"You should see him when he's angry," Kwame replied, the moon catching a twinkle in his eye.

We made camp, awaiting a cold morning that would potentially alter the past and future by our actions in the present.

I awoke to the sound of Celine and Kwame arguing, and wiped my eyes on my sleeve, rousing myself from my bedroll to investigate.

Celine was completing the finishing touches on a huge, intricately designed circle etched into the ground with some of the blue orichalcum that we had brought from the undercity. It was staggeringly complex, with dazzling spirals and runes that were dizzying, and I wondered at how she was able to complete such a complicated design while we were sleeping. Kwame was surveying her work, his arms folded in front of him, the dragon at his back. Somehow, Zzethromandus had touched down in the night without waking me or Belinda.

"What's going on?" I asked, reading the tension.

The shadowmancer tipped his swarthy chin in Celine's direction. "She thinks she can do everything."

I squinted, not understanding. "What do you mean?"

Celine rose in the middle of the teleportation circle, her hands on her broad hips. "I *think* I can bring the dragons here with you after you wake them up," she corrected Kwame, admiring her handiwork.

This was big news, given that we hadn't found a solution for that particular hurdle. "What changed?" I asked evenly.

"*Nothing* changed," Kwame emphasized, unfolding his arms in disgust. "It will take a lot out of her, with not much left to cast us back in time."

"There is not much time left," Zzethromandus added unhelpfully.

"Wait," I said, catching something in Kwame's explanation. "*Us*? You're returning to the past with me and Belinda?"

The shadowmancer nodded solemnly. "I must. Unless you have somehow learned how to lead a squad of shadow dragons into battle without my knowing of it?"

I shook my head sheepishly. "What will that

mean for the version of you that exists in my time?" I struggled to find the right words to capture my meaning. "Like, what will happen to younger Kwame?"

The high auric chuckled, his earlier ire dissipating somewhat. "The Kwame from your time is hardly young, Eskander. And he will be replaced by me."

I decided not to press the issue, given that thirty years didn't seem very long indeed for someone who was centuries old. "What about Celine, then?"

The woman shook her head, wiping her hands against one another to free them from dirt and blue dust. "No, thank you," she said firmly. "I'd prefer for young Celine to have a better future than the one I have endured."

"Young Celine will have no future at all if you perish by overextending yourself," Kwame scolded her, his voice full of reproach.

Belinda, who had heard the commotion, trotted up to join us. "Is that a possibility?"

"The human is weak," Zzethromandus offered.

"I am *not* weak," Celine protested, her brown cheeks flushing for the first time I had seen since entering the future. "The spells will take a lot out of me, but so be it. Once Eskander's been sent back in time, *old* Celine won't exist anyway."

The chronomancer spoke with brutal finality, and Kwame relented, stalking to one of the blue orichalcum packs and muttering in a language that was unfamiliar to me.

By midday, we were ready, and Celine stood at the edge of the teleportation circle, a heavy wind whipping her loose clothing about her. I took a moment to check in with Gloric and let him know of our timing in case something went awry, and he confirmed that he had secured the ceridium necessary to create a magical explosion of sorts that would provide for our route home.

Celine organized our group in the circle with Zzethromandus at its heart and me, Kwame, and Belinda at the apexes of a triangle around him. She began to cast, fist-sized gems of blue orichalcum at her feet, and I felt the world shift as the spirals and runes that surrounded us came to life. Suffused with an azure radiance, the ground rumbled as Celine's voice rose, taking on multiple harmonies caressing a persistent melody that spoke of time, space, and everything in between.

There was a blinding flash, and I covered my eyes with my arm, feeling a familiar sense of vertigo as we were transported thousands of miles in an instant. I fell to my knees, retching, feeling warm grass beneath me and an oppressive, humid heat. I looked up, my vision swaying, to find myself in a wet, green forest, a gigantic stone pyramid looming above me.

I had read about these structures in school, sacred sites of a Mayan civilization that had prospered centuries prior to our time. Celine had teleported us to within miles of Uaxactun, Guatemala, the resting place of Achivverrus, a shadow dragon that was many centuries younger than the venerable Zzethromandus. I lumbered to my feet, attempting to steady myself, and seeing Belinda's prone form a few steps away from me. Staggering drunkenly over to her, I grabbed the troll by her elbow, helping her stand.

"That was terrible," she said, wiping her mouth of spittle and looking greener than usual.

I nodded, scanning the area for Kwame and Zzethromandus, who had appeared in an open space next to the pyramid, which was crumbling and covered in moss. If the shadowmancer or dragon were bothered by the teleportation, neither of them showed it.

"This way," Zzethromandus boomed, bounding into the forest.

The trees were thin enough for the hulking dragon to move in between, but his passage still tore branches from trunks and left a path of destruction in his wake. I had no idea how inhabited this area was, or how far was the international reach of the Unaligned and their redhats, but was sure that we had announced our presence in a thunderous manner.

Moving more slowly than the swift dragon, we raced through the forest to keep up, and arrived a short time later at a large stone cairn, half the size of the pyramid we had seen. When we burst through the break in the trees, Zzethromandus was already hurtling through the tomb's stone frame, stomping and swiping rocks and boulders to reveal the interior within.

"Um," I said, panting and horrified. "Isn't this holy ground to the people in this area?"

"Not here," Kwame explained, dodging a flying stone that was as big as Belinda's head. "The pyramid where we appeared is on the very edge of the sacred site. We built this place close enough that none of the locals would touch it or attempt to break it apart."

I stared at the broken cairn dubiously, catching my breath. Satisfied, Zzethromandus scuttled backwards to a corner of the clearing, cleaning bits of rock from his claws and shaking his neck like a dog.

Kwame beckoned me over, climbing a series of wobbly stones to gaze upon the interior of the cairn. Belinda followed us, drawing her sniper rifle and taking a position at the edge of the ruined structure.

I looked over the side of the cairn, and a deep pit gaped where the ground should have been. A hundred yards within, covered in dust and rocks, lay the coiled and slumbering form of a black dragon, three quarters the size of Zzethromandus' bulk.

A long, low whistle escaped Belinda's lips from behind me as she peeked into the abyss. Beneath the rubble, Achivverrus was covered in a glistening, oily film, iridescent like the colors of a soap bubble. I recognized the magical qualities of a shadowmancy spell that bound him in life but unconscious, as it was akin to the ritual that I would perform to undo it.

Kwame brushed the dust from a large, flat boulder that overlooked the pit, inviting me to stand atop it with an unobstructed view of the dragon beneath. I cleared my throat, nervously removing a piece of blue orichalcum from my pack, and with a glance at Achivverrus' sleeping form, began my incantation.

It was halting, inelegant, and awkward, but I warmed to the ritual as I performed it, gripping the magical stone in one hand while making the arcane gestures with the other. My voice was low but strong as I chanted, and I looked to Kwame more than once to confirm that I was performing the incantation correctly. The shadowmancer was solemn and calculating, nodding here and there or making a wordless clarification, his dark hands flashing.

Rivulets of sweat beaded down my face as the ritual reached its apex, my voice dry and raspy but holding firm. I shouted the final words of the spell, casting my hands towards the pit and throwing the blue orichalcum, now the size of a skipping stone, its magic nearly spent, onto the sleeping dragon.

The gem hit the film encasing the beast, passing through it with a similar resistance to a stone falling through a pond's surface. The ritual complete, the magical covering froze in place, its oily texture becoming solid ice, and then shattered, its brilliantly colored mosaic dissipating into dust.

Achivverrus, centuries unconscious from a magic-induced slumber, rippled from horn to tail, shuddering with such great force that I had to steady myself against the precariously perched rocks beneath me. The dragon reared its head backwards, craning its powerful neck and emitting a great bellow that shook as mightily as its movement had a moment before. It opened its large, yellow eyes, its nictitating membranes sliding sideways to reveal snakelike vertical pupils the size of my hands.

Then, without warning, it jumped in the air, lifting it clean of the pit and fixing me with a terrible gaze that spoke of murderous intent.

Before I could react, Achivverrus tumbled to the side, struck with incredible force by the onrushing Zzethromandus. I watched in astonishment as the dragons cartwheeled, scrapping and scrabbling at each other until the elder pinned his younger brother to the forest floor, a huge claw at his throat and broken trees underneath.

"Siblings," Kwame chuckled.

"I guess that's what he's here for," Belinda said breathlessly, eyeing Zzethromandus' incredible ferocity in wonder.

I slumped to the rocks below me, utterly exhausted.

*****

The second and third rituals passed in similar fashion to the first, and I was grateful for Zzethromandus' presence as we awoke his younger sisters, Korrastuus and Hokkozeratus. The former was located within a forgotten mountain stronghold in the Balkans, and the latter, deep within the forests of the Congo. Both were summarily irritated at being awoken, and required forceful persuasion from their elder brother to play nice with their unwanted visitors. Dragons were particular about their sleep, I presumed.

I grew in confidence with each ritual casting, etching the ancient phrases and gestures into my mind and feeling the power from the blue orichalcum course through me unfettered. It was an exhilarating sensation, and I realized unequivocally that what magic the world had uncovered with the advent of ceridium was paltry to that which was present during the time of the Masters of Shadow.

The constant teleportation and spellcasting was a drain on our physical resources, requiring rest and recuperation in between each trip, and by the time of our return from Hokkozeratus' forest cave, a week had passed since we had ventured through Celine's first portal to Achivverrus' tomb. The dragons had taken to patrolling the skies above, which I didn't love, given that we were fugitives and were no more than a stone's throw from Unaligned power in San Francisco. I was anxious to get moving, not only because of the constant threat of redhats to the south and the errant technodragon above, but also to return to my own time.

Despite her protests, Celine needed time to restore her strength before attempting the final casting to send us back in time. The ordinarily energetic woman looked old beyond her years, and frail, with circles under her eyes that hadn't been present a week before. She waved off any concern about her livelihood, expressing that after she completed the last spell, her condition wouldn't matter, but I still worried for her.

A nagging inquiry tugged at my mind, and I voiced it during a quiet space of downtime while we were waiting for Celine to recuperate. Kwame and I had been continuing my shadowmancy training, building upon my knowledge of the ritual to suit more practical combat circumstances while Zzethromandus watched on with disinterest.

"What do you know about entromancy?" I asked, wiping the sweat from my forehead after completing a particularly challenging spell that would allow me to take the form of a shadow for a short period of time.

Kwame met my question with one of his own. "The enchantments that the Destroyer once employed?"

I nodded, remembering the first time I had encountered Agrid, in Alina's sports bar. With a couple of bizarre gesticulations, he had opened a tear in the universe and brought terrible destruction upon us. In each of my meetings with him, he had shown mastery in what Gloric had called "entromancy," a school of magic that depended on chaos to enact harmful spells in a kind of butterfly effect. It was frightening in its potency, particularly because it didn't seem to draw upon ceridium like other forms of mancy.

"We had it, in our time," Kwame said, his voice more haunted than wistful, "although the Masters of Shadow called it by a different name."

"Chaos magic," Zzethromandus rumbled, listening for once with intent. "It is a type of blood magic, drawing upon the caster's life force to disastrous effect."

That caught my attention. "Is there a counter to it?"

"No," Kwame said firmly. "It does not obey the same laws of magic as the other schools do."

"How does one combat it, then?" I asked, concerned that even if we were able to travel back in time with dragons at our back, the entromancer's magic may still prove a force too overwhelming with which to contend.

"Kill the mage," Zzethromandus said plainly, examining a foreclaw.

I did my best not to roll my eyes at a dragon.

"Sure, but how?"

"Be better than him," Kwame said honestly, receiving a snort of approval from Zzethromandus. "Short of that, prolong the battle as long as possible. Each spell will consume his physical resources, until only a husk remains."

I stared at the pair, considering. If entromancy did indeed require the caster's life force instead of another magical source, it did stand to reason that if I were to goad Agrid into casting spell after spell without rest, I could wear the low auric down enough for him to become vulnerable.

It was the only weakness of his that I had come across, and I was running out of time to prepare.

SIGIL'S LOG 1.2.224:
THE ORICHITE AGE

Halyfax stormed out of the portal and into her summoning chamber in a huff, venting a frustration that she had been unwilling to express in the cagey summit. Apprentices scattered as she appeared among them, their dark robes fluttering as they sought to escape her ire. The mistress of Shade Island was not known for being overly emotive, and her sudden, fuming arrival was alarming.

Her own island keep, a league from what would be known in centuries to come as the west coast of North America, could not have been more different from the meeting place of the Masters of Shadow. It was temperate, often sun-soaked, with a pleasantly cool breeze that smelled of salt and seaweed. The high orichite threw back the hood of her cloak, dripping rain water from her previous swamp location as she stalked out of the pleasantly sunlit round chamber and out onto an adjacent balcony.

The stone terrace led to a spiraling exterior staircase that circumnavigated the tower of her keep and afforded her with a magnificent view of the Pacific Ocean. Waves crested and fell, dashing dramatically against the barnacled rocks that ringed the foundation of the keep far below. Seagulls squatted among the stones, filling the salty air with their cries and taking to the sky when a particularly large wave sprayed foam in their direction. Here and there, a sea lion played, dark and distinct against the indigo waves that were gold-tipped from the afternoon sun.

Halyfax saw none of the beauty that ringed her keep as she stomped up the stone steps, wringing out the sleeves of her robes as she circled the tower to its apex. She spoke a word of power as she reached the warded door to her private quarters, and it flew open as she approached, swinging forcefully inwards to a thickly carpeted room within.

She stepped inside, dripping on a richly colored, tasseled rug, and spoke again, setting the hearth in the room's huge fireplace to flame. The door closed behind her, and the shadowmancer exchanged her heavy robes for a simple but functional tunic and trousers. Light poured in from open slats within the tower's heavy stone walls, warded by magic against the elements, and the room was quickly warmed by the large hearth.

Halyfax strode to her lectern, a simple wooden stand that supported a bulky tome held open with a cloth bookmark. She withdrew a glimmering piece of blue orichalcum from a cubby carved into the lectern's wood, reciting a spell from the book that she hadn't already committed to memory. Her brow creased in concentration as her words took form, drawing upon the magical stones to create a palate of shadow in front of the lectern, shimmering and murky in the bright room.

The shadow coalesced into a rectangle, wavering and wispy at the edges but substantial. The spell complete, it awaited her command.

The high orichite hesitated, unsure of her chosen course of action but unwilling to make a decision without having more information to consider. It was impolite, if not downright hostile, to scry upon another Master of Shadow without their knowledge, but Halyfax could think of no other way to obtain the information that she desired.

"Kwame Daigan," she said at last, her blonde eyebrows relaxing as she made her choice.

The shadow window shifted, forming itself into a curtain of sorts, roiling first into fluid shapes that in turn shimmered into black and grey images, crystalline in their clarity even without color.

Halyfax's breath caught in her throat as she witnessed, deep within shadow, the dark orichite high on a mountainside, scrabbling among the snow-capped rocks as he conversed with a shadow dragon that was at least a quarter of the size of her island keep. The drake – Zzethromandus, if she recalled his name correctly – took one step up the mountain for Kwame's every hundred, unconcerned by the blizzard. The pair seemed oddly companionable, conversing about something as they traversed the white ridge of a peak.

Without warning, the shadow dragon swung his huge, serpentine neck in Halyfax's direction, pinning her with his great emerald eyes as his innate magic unraveled her spell with a *pop*. Halyfax skipped backwards, nearly tumbling the lectern, as the scene abruptly faded from view.

What she had done was more dangerous than expected, she realized, although in her mind, it had still proved to be fruitful. She had to see Kwame for herself, cavorting with dragons, to confirm Intari's claims about his plans to learn from them and enact the ritual that would preserve their shadowmancy. With the vision from her scrying spell, she was confident that the elder troll's assertions were valid, along with her admonition that such a ritual would draw upon their life force to complete, sacrificing themselves for the preservation of their art.

Therein lay the conflict, Halyfax thought ruefully. The Masters of Shadow, herself included, were an egocentric sort, dedicated to their own survival as much as to the safeguarding of shadowmancy. They would do anything to preserve their magical lore, but the idea of throwing themselves into the void to prevent an unproven threat would not garner much support, even from the likes of the well-meaning Fey and Harald, among others.

Still, Halyfax trusted Kwame's ability, if not his judgment. The shadowmancer had proven himself to be one of the most powerful among them, but also sympathetic to the inscrutable idea of a shared community between the orichites and humans. What drove him towards such a belief was unfathomable to Halyfax, but everyone was allowed a vice, she supposed.

Perhaps, she thought to herself slyly, picking

up another piece of blue orichalcum from the lectern, there was a way to alter the ritual. It was not inconceivable that the dragons, wise in the ways of shadowmancy as they may be, only understood a subset of the tapestry of magic that Kwame intended to employ. If Intari's explanation of Kwame's warnings were to be believed, then within a century, the humans would have depleted the earth's reserves of blue orichalcum to dangerous levels. The Masters of Shadow would be able to preserve their lore in the bodies of the dragons, who would roam until a prophesied time, a millennium in the future, when blue orichalcum resurfaced. Shadowmancy would flourish again by some mechanism that was unknown to Halyfax, but was apparently spoken about convincingly by the dragons.

The logic was flimsy to Halyfax's analytical mind, but she didn't take the drakes' warning, filtered as it was through Kwame and Intari, lightly. She resolved to watch, and wait, and plan, using the current time afforded to her to determine if there was a way to pervert the ritual, preserving the life force of the Masters of Shadow so that they could be resurrected when indeed blue orichalcum appeared after its depletion.

The shadowmancer shuddered, recalling the predatory, knowing look of Zzethromandus as the dragon shattered her spell. Then she began casting, using the blue orichalcum in her fist to send a message across oceans and forests to Intari.

SEVEN

"The Masters of Shadow were not paragons of virtue; nor should they serve as examples of virtuous mancy conduct. They sought to preserve orichite history in a manner that many questioned, and time will determine whether their actions were just, or merely prideful foolishness."

-Kwame Daigan, Master of Shadow

Nothing about the chronomancy spell to send us home went according to plan.

I woke with a start on the predetermined morning of our departure, a buzzing in my ear alerting me that I had a call waiting on my digitab.

"Yeah?" I muttered groggily, not having a clue who would be able to access my line on the network in this time period, save for Gloric from the past.

"Eskander?" a familiar voice chirped tentatively in my ear.

I shook my head, trying to clear it of sleep. "Mom?" I asked incredulously.

"Eskander!" my mother shouted more forcefully, her accented voice dripping with reprimand. "What's this I hear about you traveling to Fuji and not telling anyone? We've been worried sick!"

"What," I said, baffled. "I'm not in Fuji, mom. I've come to the *future*."

"What?" it was my mother's turn to be confused. "Hang on."

"Give me the digitab, Beybun," a stern voice echoed through my earpiece as my father jumped on the line. "Eskander? Do you know how worried your mother and I have been? The people at NIGHT told us you were dead, and even Alina-"

"I'm sorry, dad, things have been kind of crazy. I'll explain it all when I get back."

"And when will that be?" my father asked imperiously.

"Soon," I said, hoping that it was true. A thought occurred to my waking brain. "Dad, how are you calling me?"

"Your gnome friend got in touch with us this morning, telling us you were in Fuji and that he would connect us through his network."

"It's not Fuji, dad," I scolded, getting irritated. "Does Alina-"

"Alina called us this morning as well," my father interrupted. "She sounded very angry, Eskander. *Very* angry."

I lifted my face towards the sky in frustration, vying to get even with Gloric for contacting my family after I had asked him not to. In my peripheral vision, I noticed Kwame hurrying towards me, concern written across his ebony skin.

"Dad, I've got to go," I said, hastily pulling on my gear. "Can you call Alina? Tell her I'm sorry and will be in touch with her soon?"

"Alina!" my father guffawed incredulously. "What about *us*? How do you think we-"

"Got to go, dad!" I repeated, clicking the line closed. I turned to Kwame. "What's going on?"

"We have to move," the shadowmancer said urgently, rousing Belinda from her bedroll a few feet away from me. The troll jumped up like a soldier, reaching for her weapons.

I looked at the time on my lens display. We were due to connect with Gloric in an hour to prepare for the ritual on both sides of time.

"Redhats," Kwame said, reading the hesitation on my face. "Celine's allies tipped us off to movement in our direction, less than an hour ago."

I nodded, checking my gear and trailing after the high auric as he sped back towards the teleportation circle, Belinda following closely behind us. I clicked open my line with Gloric.

"Nightpath," he greeted me comfortably.

"I asked you to keep my presence here a secret, Gloric," I admonished him.

"I said I wouldn't mention it."

"You lied."

"I'm the Sigil, not a saint," the gnome sounded irritated. "What do you want?"

"We may be moving up the timeline," I explained, breaking into a run as I saw Celine already beginning her casting as the four dragons alighted gracefully at cardinal points at the edges of the runed circle. "Can you create your technomancy explosion thing in, say, five minutes?"

"Holy hell, Nightpath," the Sigil groused, his exasperation with me rising. "I'm in the middle of breakfast!"

"Skip it," I shouted, sprinting as I saw saucer-shaped gliders appear at the southern edge of the ruins. "Five minutes, Gloric!"

I closed the line as I skidded to a stop just inside the teleportation circle, looking to Kwame, who was as close to wringing his hands as I had seen the normally stoic high auric.

"How long?" I asked, gesturing towards Celine, who looked thin and pale but was confidently moving through the intricacies of her chronomancy spell. An entire pile of blue orichalcum lay strewn around her waifish form, glowing as it depleted itself to power her incantation.

"Too long," Kwame replied, anguish in his voice. I understood his distress, given the amount of time and effort we had all spent for this particular moment in time, himself and Zzethromandus especially.

The dragon wasn't willing to encounter the situation lying down. Giving a great bellow at his newly awakened kin, Zzethromandus launched himself into the air, speeding southwards like an arrow, his siblings close on his heels. The redhat gliders visibly shook, even at this distance, as they took in the sight of the magical beasts barreling towards them.

"Dragon!" Kwame called after Zzethromandus, sounding like a parent admonishing a wayward child. "You need to be *here* for us to leave!"

If the elder dragon heard Kwame's squawking, he paid no mind. The beasts tore into the midst of a score or more gliders, rending at them with their wickedly long claws or tossing them to ground with a powerful flick of their jaws.

A handful of the gliders curved out of their destructive path, making a beeline for our teleportation circle. We were an obvious target in the middle of the blasted land, sitting ducks without protection.

Belinda responded the quickest, sighting down her sniper rifle as I drew my ceridium wand. The troll squeezed the trigger on her weapon, and one of the gliders fell to the earth as its driver took a ceridium bullet to the face.

Four more gliders sped in our direction, and I loosed a shot from the wand, a cobalt ray lasering through the air and scything through another vehicle. The glider split in half like a sandwich, spilling its contents to the dirt and grass, black-clad humans wearing silly-looking angular red helmets and armed with weird alien weaponry of their own.

The other three gliders were upon us in seconds, firing at us with triangular-shaped blasters affixed to their chassis. There was nowhere for us to hide, and no rocks or trees to use as cover, so we skipped away, trying to keep within the teleportation circle in case Celine finished her spell.

Kwame worked like a demon, grabbing bits of blue orichalcum and using them to deflect shots from the gliders out of the air as they beaded towards the stationary Celine, who was unable to move as she concentrated on her spell. One beam got past his defense, blasting through the woman's calf, but she held her attention, her face screwed up in pain and determination.

I fired another ray from my wand, and the

stupid thing sputtered, its ammunition spent. I threw it to the ground in disgust as Belinda took out another of the drivers, just as the dragons returned from their foray, several more gliders at their backs.

Zzethromandus and his siblings landed heavily in their positions at the tips of the circle just as Celine finished her spell, the remainder of the blue orichalcum at her feet turning from solid rock into a swirling liquid and finally, a spiraling gas as the chronomancer's incantation took form. The dragons roared as one, shaking the earth as the gliders peppered the teleportation circle with rays of death, passing through our incorporeal forms as Celine's magic transported us from the future into the past. The lasers rent the woman's body as she collapsed, utterly spent, at the edge of the circle that faded from our sight.

My travel through time was similar to and somehow different from the trip that had brought me to the future. I had gotten used to the feeling of disorientation and vertigo, and felt a sense of familiarity as I approached the past. In an instant, I experienced a multitude of visions, most of which remain fractured and enigmatic to me.

I saw a dystopian future, even more distant and apocalyptic than the one from which I had just come, all angles and shadows as broken, skyscraping buildings were patrolled by lifeless machines that pulsed in red and blue. I saw a past, far removed from my own time, with armies of orichites and humans marching to war, pennants waving as they joined in battle with sword and spell. Dragons of different stripes and colors dipped and swooped, raining carnage amidst battlefields that churned with instruments of destruction.

Deep within that bygone past, I saw King Thog'run II, manacled and pilloried, a prisoner in some ancient dungeon and awaiting the executioner's axe.

I jolted to awareness as I hit the ground, my hands full of grass and my body shaking from the time shift and adrenaline from the fight with the gliders. Bile filled my throat and I swallowed hard, swaying, fighting the nausea as the most incredible scent hit my nostrils.

A cool sea breeze had made its way over the forests of the Marin Headlands and caressed my face on a bright blue morning, the sun warming the spaces between the trees to send wet dew curling lazily towards the heavens.

Less than a year after the Three Factions War and the technodragon blast that sent me into the future, I was home.

A welcome party of sorts was waiting for us, and my throat tightened with emotion as my eyes cleared and I saw a pair of all-terrain AG cruisers, positioned next to a weird, machine-like contraption that looked like a cross between a mainframe and a grain mill. Gloric, his hands still extended towards the apparatus and glowing with an azure fire, took an involuntary step backwards as my party appeared, the four dragons bucking and tossing their necks as they adjusted from the time travel.

"Holy smokes," a gruff voice said, and I saw Vasshka "Doubleshot" Lestrage, the king's dwarven revolutionary and my friend, standing on the hood of one of the cruisers with her eyes wide and mouth open. A lit cigar dropped from her face, forgotten.

Behind her in the cruiser was a much younger Tribe Achebe than the one I had seen recently, bedecked in his leathers with a punky haircut and a bevy of earrings that accentuated his long, high auric ears. He was murmuring something to Alina Hadzic, my sort-of-girlfriend that was known by most as the Pitcher, who was standing in front of the vehicle with her arms crossed, staring at me. A shaggy-looking Buster, her wolf companion, barked angrily from the passenger seat next to Tribe, unnerved by the sudden presence of the huge dragons.

Alina was flanked on either side by the Alyawarre siblings, the big and burly Andrew looking just as astonished as Doubleshot, and the younger, happy-looking Celine with eyes as wide as saucers. She, too, would have participated in providing a conduit for the spell that brought us back, I knew, but she looked vibrant and youthful, wholly at odds with the older Celine that had just found her demise in front of me a moment before.

I pushed the future, past, and everything in between from my mind and stumbled to Alina, clutching at her coat and throwing my normal sense of propriety to the winds as I pulled her to me in a long, passionate kiss and embrace. She melted in my arms for half of it, then stiffened, shoving me away with the strength of an athlete and punching me in the face.

"What the hell!" I complained, holding my jaw. I wavered, feeling the time travel catch up with me as my lens display exploded with unread notifications from the past.

"What the hell, *you!*" she retorted. "How come we had to hear from Gloric that you weren't dead?"

"She's right," Doubleshot quipped, having recovered from her surprise at the dragons.

"Eskander," Kwame said cheerily from behind me, "won't you introduce us to your friends?"

Reluctantly, I introduced my companions to Kwame, Belinda, Zzethromandus, Achivverrus, Korrastuus, and Hokkozeratus, the dragons having little interest in making pleasantries and taking to the skies almost immediately to patrol our location. Belinda's timesick gaze lingered on Tribe, the high auric's youthful appearance jarringly incongruous with the dour Duc that we had seen more recently, but the sniper looked queasy and said nothing about their time together.

We had precious little time to catch up as my friends had infiltrated into hostile territory to meet us, phantoms on the network due to some careful work on Gloric's part. The technomancy spell he had cast using the weird mechanical contraption would have undoubtedly drawn the attention of Agrid's technodragons, who were never far from the forests above Aurichome.

We didn't have long to wait. Not a quarter of an hour after we had appeared, a thunderous roar from Zzethromandus alerted us of the danger that approached.

Aware of our presence, the Unaligned had scrambled to organize their forces, leading the charge with their awful, abominable technodragons that had been the bane of

Aurichome and its king.

Zzethromandus alighted on the ground with a rumble, tossing his horned head towards me and Kwame. "The entromancer is here," he said. "Come."

I looked at Kwame incredulously. "Um," I hedged, my mouth dry.

"Come on!" he yelled, already running towards the dragon.

I looked at Alina and the others, preparing for the oncoming battle as Agrid's assassin foot soldiers and cruisers appeared at the edge of the forest, intercepted by aurikar warriors that had been lying in wait for them.

The Pitcher's ire had softened since she had hit me, and she responded to my yearning glance with a tentative smile of her own. "Come back soon," she said, handing me a ceridium pistol.

"I promise," I gulped, holstering the weapon at my belt, opposite my nightblade.

I raced to Kwame, who helped me spring to a spot between the ridges on the dragon's back, lashing me to a bony spike with a cord that he had produced from somewhere. I held on for dear life as Zzethromandus sprung into the sky, well above the canopy, to join his siblings.

I would have been willing to take ten more trips through time instead of riding on the back of the dragon. The beast bucked and spun, dipping and rising with every beat of his wings, and my makeshift harness did little to ensure my safety. Zzethromandus swirled, joining his kin in a predatory circle around our battlefield, and affording us a view of the entire North Bay.

Far below, my companions joined the battle

in earnest, their cruisers jittering over the landscape as the telltale blue sparks of Vasshka's ceridium pistols and Belinda's sniper rifle fired at encroaching Unaligned soldiers. I could see Alina's ceridium orb as well, flashing through the forest only to return to her grasp, and Gloric's tiny figure stopping Agrid's cruisers in their tracks as the technomancer took control of their ceruchip cores from a distance. I was sure that I saw the backs of Tribe's and Andrew's heads as they drove the others in a frighteningly dangerous route among the trees, one or both of them augmented in reflexes by Celine's magic.

As we rose into the blue sky, I saw the technodragons, triangulating on our position from whatever unlucky locations they had been haunting. From the south came several cerucopters and other air vehicles to meet them, easily recognizable as being of NIGHT make.

I could have kissed Gloric as surely as I had Alina. The gnome had undoubtedly gotten in touch with Madge, my old compatriot and the Inquisitor General of the NIGHT headquarters on Alcatraz. She had sent support to see justice done for the atrocities committed against both her organization and Aurichome months before.

The NIGHT vehicles, their metal chassis glinting in the bright sunlight, were met in force by Unaligned air fighters that rose from the forests below, ominous and ugly like cockroaches. I didn't have time to consider the impending dogfight as Zzethromandus swerved at Kwame's behest, breaking formation with his siblings to engage one of the technodragons that was racing at us from a higher altitude.

The horrid beasts were a mismatched pastiche of rotting sinew and foul machinery, fueled by ceridium and an unholy life force. Their shark-like, lifeless cobalt eyes stared predatorily ahead as their riders commanded their actions from metallic harnesses affixed to the backs of their hideous skeletons.

The one in front of us was helmed by a dwarf, whom I recognized as being Ghela, Agrid's technomancer that had resurrected the first technodragon in the Sigil's sanctuary, murdering the old Sigil and stealing his life force in the process. My trepidation at riding Zzethromandus forgotten, I yelled in pure fury, angry at the turn of events that had led us to this confrontation.

The technodragon responded in kind, heaving its hollow chest to vomit its foul, magical breath in our direction. An electric ceridium beam, thick as a redwood tree, shot towards us, crackling with deathly energy.

Zzethromandus was quicker than the undead monstrosity, jerking to the side as the technodragon's breath skimmed past us and tore through a line of trees below, setting them aflame. I held on with both hands as the elder dragon continued his climb, avoiding the technodragon's bony head and latching onto its flank with his foreclaws.

Ghela attempted to move the beast's head towards us for another blast, but Zzethromandus had cunningly positioned us behind the technodragon's writhing neck, pulling the evil thing downwards from its original trajectory. The technomancer atop its back jolted wildly, her eyes wide with panic.

"Now! Shoot!" Kwame said from in front of me, riding Zzethromandus' squirming form effortlessly.

I reluctantly released one of my tightly-gripping hands from the dragon's neck as we plummeted, fumbling for the ceridium pistol at my waist. I did my best to sight down the scope, firing erratically towards the dwarf, who hid behind the railing of the harness.

"Useless!" Kwame complained in disgust. The shadowmancer hurled himself from Zzethromandus' back, climbing up the dragon's neck like a mountain goat and hurtling through the air towards the technodragon, his foot extended horizontally. Ghela, rising from her crouch in an attempt to regain control of the monstrosity beneath her, caught Kwame's jump kick in her horned temple, tumbling arse-over-teakettle across the lip of the harness, her body dashing against the trees below.

Its rider dealt with, the technodragon continued to dive, writhing as Zzethromandus repositioned himself over its back. Kwame clambered over the elder dragon's shoulder and back in front of me as the beast snapped its jaws around the technodragon's neck, rearing backwards and tearing the monster's spine from its torso.

The technodragon gave an evil gasp as the unnatural life force escaped its broken body, the blue fire in its eyes extinguishing as the thing became no more than a tangled mess of rotten flesh and metal. Zzethromandus dropped the empty husk unceremoniously, letting out a feral howl as he beat his wings against his own flank, taking us clear of the onrushing trees.

My stomach hit my throat as we gained altitude quickly, and we leveled out to see Achivverrus and Korrastuus squaring off against another two technodragons and a pair of cerucopters. The Unaligned vehicles' weapon fire skipped off the dragons' armored black scales harmlessly, but a blast from one of the technodragons' terrible breaths seared through Achivverrus' shoulder, rendering his wing useless and sending him careening into the trees. His sister roared in fury, spitting black fire at the cerucopters and liquefying them utterly before spearing towards the exposed neck of the technodragon.

Simultaneously, Hokkozeratus had completed her circle and came charging into the fray, snapping her jaws in the hopes of disabling the rider on the second technodragon's back. The unnatural beast swerved, protecting the technomancer at its helm, but exposing its putrid belly. Hokkozeratus seized the opportunity, turning her charge into a pounce and burying her hind claws into the monstrosity's abdomen with a shriek.

Zzethromandus' flight took us in a sharp turn to meet a new threat, and I saw Agrid, perched behind yet another of his technomancer lieutenants on a fourth technodragon. The entromancer's crimson coat whipped behind him in the wind, his crackling ebony and blue spear mixing with the undead life force emanating from the beast below him in a macabre display of power.

The elder dragon below me gave a snort of derision and dipped, attempting to goad the technodragon in a similar manner as he had done with the first. The monster took the bait, expelling its breath weapon with terrible precision, but Zzethromandus was again the quicker, riding the current of the wind out of harm's way and towards the technodragon's throat.

Agrid the Destroyer was ready for us, completing an entromancy spell that I had experienced previously, throwing seeds to the earth below as a sharp whistle escaped his lips. A gash in the void opened in front of Zzethromandus' lurching form, bolts of crimson pelting the great beast with magical hellfire.

The dragon roared in pain, his scales smoldering with evil flame and one of his great eyes immediately swelling shut. He hurtled heedlessly into the technodragon, tearing and clawing blindly as the monster bucked and whirled.

I could do nothing but hold on as we fell, dragons and riders all, to the forest below, smashing through the trees painfully as the two beasts pivoted and scraped in their violent embrace. I grabbed Kwame's arm as even he lost his purchase on Zzethromandus' back, dropping my pistol to hastily grab a ceridium capsule from my pocket and spit the words of a spell.

The dragons hit the forest floor with an earthquake, shattering bones, trees, and hastily retreating cruisers as the beasts continued to tumble. I released my spell, which had shifted Kwame and me into shadows that glided harmlessly down the trunk of a great redwood, transporting us to relative safety away from the battling dragons.

Kwame looked at me appraisingly as we caught our breath from the encounter, the sounds of battle assaulting us from every direction. "Thank you," he offered, staring into the distance.

"You taught me that," I said, following his gaze to see Agrid, his blood-colored coat torn but his body covered in protective, hexagonal quicksilver armor, stalking through the forest towards us.

EIGHT

"Contrary to popular belief, time is not our enemy. The hubris inherent in auric and human nature, however, very much is."
                    -Gloric Vunderfel, the Sigil of Sparks

The entromancer prowled towards us, outnumbered and unconcerned, his spear spitting and crackling with blue energy.

Kwame and I spread out wordlessly, understanding intuitively that our teamwork would be an asset against the dangerous low auric. Agrid the Betrayer continued to march, his beady black eyes calculating against the ashen white of his skin.

"It's come to this," I called, trying to distract him.

"So it has," he shouted in his nondescript voice, taking in the sight of Kwame curiously before looking in my direction.

"Did you get what you wanted out of all of this?" I waved a hand to take in the carnage and chaos, the sounds of dragons and artillery reverberating throughout the forest on fire.

Agrid kept advancing, his eyes flicking between me and the shadowmancer, assessing this new threat.

"I killed you with my own two hands," the low auric growled suspiciously, ignoring my question.

I drew a ceridium capsule from a pocket, casting a shadowmancy spell that I had learned from combining one of Kwame's teachings with an incantation of my own. A long, ropy whip made of viscous shadowstuff appeared in my hand, and I began spinning it in a low, threatening loop.

"Not exactly," I quipped.

To my left, Kwame continued to circle, attempting to put Agrid in between us. The entromancer looked at him mildly, then turned his attention back to me.

"Aurichome is mine, and the City belongs to the Unaligned," Agrid said confidently. "Your apparent resurrection is inconsequential."

"Maybe," I said, buying time for Kwame to get into position. "But at least I haven't sold my race to fascists to settle an old grudge."

The entromancer grinned, his modest tusks sparkling against his quicksilver body armor. "Don't waste your breath, Nightpath. You won't goad me as you have done before. I chose my allegiances long ago."

I returned his smile unironically, as Thog'run's voice from an age ago echoed in my head. *I think the entromancy has corrupted him,* the king had said as we had attempted to unravel the strands of Agrid's betrayal in coordination with the Unaligned. *One who cavorts with chaos cannot help but be tainted by it.*

Here, in the midst of a pitched battle to

determine the fate of two nations and the aurics and humans that swore fealty to them, I at last understood what the entromancer stood for, and what drove him. It mattered little that his benefactors in the Unaligned would see him as a pawn in their machinations, or that his counterpart in Karthax espoused a message of hate that did violence to the underraces, including the aurikar royal family, of which he was technically a part.

Agrid had once chosen an exclusionary, separatist ideal as his mission, believing that aurics and humans could only coexist in contention, or not at all. He used the conflict between them as a guiding light that became twisted with his deeper involvement with entromancy, shrouding himself in chaos and hate as Thog'run exiled him from Aurichome, and thus from his own family.

All that mattered to Agrid the Betrayer, now in this moment, was to sow chaos wherever he found order, continuing a pattern of anarchy and confusion even if it brought harm to the aurics of San Francisco at the hands of Karthax and the Unaligned.

I felt my smile dip into a glower, angry that the actions of one person could cause harm to so many people. My shadow whip came out of its circle just as the entromancer stalked within range, and I sent it spiraling forward to lash soundlessly like a striking snake.

Agrid caught the whip on his ceridium-laced spear, allowing it to coil around its blade before shattering it into dust with a flick of his wrist. Kwame used the diversion to suddenly bolt towards the low auric, tumbling at the last moment to spring with an extended fist at the entromancer's tusked face. The Destroyer sidled backwards, knocking the blow away with a crack of his spear, and he tossed droplets of blood from where his long nails had covertly pierced his palm, stamping his foot and growling in unison. Sharp, scarlet arrows took shape in front of his extended hand, threatening Kwame at point blank range.

Quicker than thought, the ancient auric flattened himself against the dirt floor, allowing the bolts to fly past him and tear through the underbrush. I drew my nightblade, casting another spell that transported me through the shadows and directly within range of the melee. I exited the ether with a two-handed chop downwards, forcing Agrid to raise his spear to receive it or be cleaved in two.

The entromancer moved with the strike, rolling his spear as it crackled against my nightblade and thrusting its ceridium-caressed blade towards my face. I ducked, spinning and releasing a cross-wise slash that struck him in the torso, shattering the quicksilver armor but without doing real harm.

Kwame sprung to his feet, flipping on a horizontal axis as he brought the top of his foot down towards Agrid's head. The entromancer parried the strike easily, twirling his spear like a baton and hitting me across the jaw and Kwame in the midsection with the same motion. I spat teeth and blood as pain exploded across my face, and Kwame fell to the earth heavily, knocked out of his spin.

Agrid grunted in satisfaction and stepped back, calling out in the voice of a raven and producing an egg from his torn coat, which he promptly stamped upon. His bizarre spell twisted the entropy of the universe to his will, re-forming his quicksilver armor, and for the briefest of moments, I saw his dull features contort in pain, using his own life force to enact the entromancy. I drove forward, heedless of the pain, slashing with renewed vigor and a ferocity that took the low auric by surprise.

He staggered backwards, catching the blows on his spear or parrying them to the side, but I caught him with a riposte that again shattered through the armor and this time, pierced one of his muscular legs.

The Destroyer growled in pain and brought the butt of his spear up under my guard to punch me in the throat, and I flew backwards, tears blurring my vision as I hit the trunk of a nearby tree. I heard, rather than saw, the entromancer cast his spell again, drawing upon his energy reserves to shield himself in chaos.

Leaves crunched in front of me as Agrid stalked in my direction, and my eyes cleared in time to see his spear poised for a killing blow. I lifted my blade, placing my hand on its blunt spine and grunting with effort as the sword caught the spear on its edge.

The pressure released immediately as Kwame materialized behind the entromancer, breaking the quicksilver armor yet again with a cracking elbow to the back of Agrid's head. Before the low auric could respond, Kwame snaked his arms around the entromancer's neck and head in a three-point choke, jumping to latch his legs around Agrid's torso like a vise. The entromancer flailed, spinning in a half-circle as his eyes bulged, unable to catch the lithe shadowmancer behind him with his spear.

Halfway to unconsciousness, Agrid threw himself against a tree, and I heard a crunch as one or more of Kwame's ribs broke beneath him. The shadowmancer loosened his grip, and Agrid took the opportunity to spring forward, turning and making a gurgling sound while extracting a rabbit's foot from his jacket and twirling it in an oval before him.

The entromancy spell drove the already-depleted low auric to his knee, but had an even more terrible effect on Kwame. Bloody, excruciating wounds appeared on the shadowmancer's battered body, and he screamed in pain, clawing at his face.

"Enough," I said, wavering to my feet with the help of the trunk behind me. The entromancer turned to meet my tremulous charge, casting his quicksilver armor spell again, the color draining from his already pallid face.

Rage, rather than technique, fueled my attacks, and the Destroyer was hard-pressed to keep up with my wild strikes. He parried and dodged, but I kept coming, my voice rising painfully in my bruised throat as I hacked away at him, destroying his armor as I accepted a glancing blow to my chest from his spear.

The entromancer used the strike to push himself away, hurriedly casting a spell that created another set of crimson arrows that sped towards me. His shoulders slumped with the effort and I sprung forward, ignoring the pain of the blood bolts as they tore through my body. I drove my nightblade in front of me, blood filling my mouth and my vision beginning to cloud.

"*ENOUGH*," I yelled thickly, pouring the last of my strength into a thrust that pierced Agrid's torso, much as it had on a windswept NIGHT tower on Alcatraz less than two years before.

This time, the tip of my blade found his heart.

I collapsed to the forest floor, allowing the waiting darkness to take me.

*****

I awoke to bright lights and sterile smells, disoriented and fearful that I had again traveled away from the present, and been deposited this time in some prison-like future. The din of medical machinery greeted my ears, and my mind slowly adjusted to what I later learned was an aurikar hospital deep within the newly reclaimed Aurichome. Alina sat by my bed, reading something on her digitab, her pitching arm slung in a bandage and the area around her right eye yellow from the remnants of a nasty bruise.

"You alright?" I croaked, my throat not quite recovered from the entromancer's attack.

The Pitcher nodded, her smiling blue eyes a beautiful sight for my weariness.

"How long?" I asked, attempting to push myself up to a sitting position and failing.

"You've been out for three days," she said, placing her digitab on a side table and helping me to sit up. "The battle lasted less than one."

I nodded, which also hurt. "Gloric and the others?"

She nodded back at me. "Not in great shape, but not as bad as you. Your family's come in from Philly and staying nearby."

I sighed, injured and exhausted beyond belief, but happy to hear that my companions were safe. "I love you," I said suddenly, whatever barriers that had prevented me from doing so earlier melting with the passage of time.

"I get that," she said, smiling again. "It's been a hard few months," she added, and her freckled face took on a haunted look that quickly vanished.

"I'm sorry," I replied, anguished at the pain I must have caused by my absence in such a troubling time, even against my volition. "When we first contacted Gloric, I just thought-"

"It's OK," Alina said, sensing my agitation. She put a firm but gentle hand on my chest. "I understand. And I love you, too."

I nodded again, closing my eyes for an eternity.

*****

A month later, I found myself standing in Aurichome's royal audience chamber, the blue-and-white carpets and drapes doing little to cheer the solemn mood that pervaded the stone room. Despite the ministrations of the queen's best terramancers and Madge's personal Daypaths, I would still require crutches for another few weeks as my body continued to heal itself after what should have been a fatal spell from Agrid. A NIGHT squad had happened upon Kwame and me, rushing our bodies to a nearby field medic. The hardy shadowmancer had already made a full recovery, and had been encouraging me for the past month, not unkindly, to keep up.

The dragons had taken up positions at the four corners of the North Bay above Aurichome for a week, warding against further Unaligned attacks with their ominous presence. With the blessing of the queen, which, apparently, they accepted, Zzethromandus and his kin flew to whatever aeries they called home to lick their wounds and recover in the case of another battle.

Unlike an awkward awards ceremony that I had been invited to in the same audience chamber some time before, this meeting was all business. Queen Fazgha Hezdottr sat on the stone throne, her tusks gleaming white against robes of blue, and her strong hands folded politely in her lap. Several courtiers and royal family members flanked her, including the crown prince, Thog'run III, and Tribe, who had exchanged his leathers for more formal state attire.

"We have known each other for far too long to prevaricate, Inquisitor General," the queen was saying emphatically, addressing Madge, my once-comrade and leader of the NIGHTs on Alcatraz.

The human nodded vigorously, her black ponytail bouncing. "Agreed, Your Highness," Madge said smoothly, "but we honestly have no leads regarding election tampering. However Karthax found himself in office, it seems the public wants him there."

"Cannot your government take him into custody on the grounds of his war crimes? He was court martialed *in absentia*!"

Madge spread her hands placatingly. "Our reach only extends so far," she said, referring to NIGHT's status as a paramilitary force. "All I can say is that although Karthax continues to be mayor of San Francisco, he's sandwiched between Aurichome and our headquarters. We'll keep tabs on him from our side, if you will as well."

Fazgha harrumphed, unsatisfied but without a better option. It was a tremulous alliance between two factions that had been at each other's throats since their respective inceptions, but now that they had a common enemy, it would have to do.

Their opponent was a strange and splintered one, given that many representatives of the so-called Unaligned had, after Agrid's defeat and Aurichome's reclamation, become vocal that they did not stand with Karthax's intolerance of aurics and siege mentality against the outside world. San Francisco remained free from aurikar and NIGHT influence, and the fate of the underrace-inhabited undercity was as yet unclear, but it seemed that many within the Unaligned had been quick to position themselves apart from the xenophobic mayor.

"Malevolence against others has a way of rearing its ugly head, some time or another," Kwame spoke aloud after Madge and her NIGHT agents had left.

The queen nodded from her throne. "Well said, shadowmancer."

"You sure I can't just kill him?" Vasshka said laconically, taking a draw from a cigar while tapping one of her pistols meaningfully.

"I like her," Belinda whispered from her

protective perch near me, her sniper rifle customarily strapped across her huge back. I had caught her eyeing the younger Tribe on more than one occasion, and wondered if she had yet taken the opportunity to speak with him about their past – or future – together.

I smirked. "You can try," I answered Doubleshot's question, having had personal experience in combat with the former Inquisitor General. "You'll have to be quicker than I was when I last fought him."

"That shouldn't be too difficult," Alina said teasingly, mirth in her eyes as she tousled Buster's mane, the wolf's large head nuzzling her hip.

"No killing," the queen said seriously, sweeping the room with an imperious, steel-eyed gaze, resting it finally on the Alyawarre siblings, who were the only two humans given free access to the aurikar palace. "There has been enough of that already."

With that, I couldn't disagree.

SIGIL'S LOG 1.2.301:
THE ORICHITE AGE

A century came and went, and Kwame's prophecy slowly came to fruition. The dark auric wouldn't take credit for the augury, protesting that all of his knowledge of the future came from prolonged discussions with the dragons, but Halyfax could see her fellow Master of Shadow's hand in what would soon take place.

The humans, short-lived compared to her kind and illiterate in the ways of life-preserving magic, had fought tooth-and-nail over their inconsequential settlements. Yet, increasingly empowered as they were from the lore they learned from neighboring orichites that looked upon them kindly, they had become even more violent, churning through blue orichalcum to power their combative spells and instruments of war. Some orichite kingdoms had responded in kind, decimating nearby human villages and even cities in the hopes of preserving the limited resource. Others had become so deeply intertwined with them as to be unrecognizable, orichites and humans living amidst one another.

Halyfax shuddered at the thought of half-tusked, half-long-eared children traipsing about once-great orichite civilizations. The humans were indeed encroaching on the homelands of her people, and even though Shade Island remained unassailable, there was no longer a question of the imminent danger posed by the other race's depletion of blue orichalcum.

The threat had escalated rapidly, at least in her estimation, although the orichite perception of time was of a different stripe than that of humans. It had taken decades of what Halyfax considered to be careful but hurried work to make her mark on the ritual that the Masters of Shadow would perform, altering it to have a slightly different but no less significant trajectory than expected.

The Masters had agreed, to a person, to undergo the ritual, sacrificing their life essence to preserve their art until a time that the dragons assured them would come to pass. Zzethromandus had identified three of his kin, among whom he would disperse the essence, preserving their knowledge of shadowmancy until blue orichalcum appeared among the world again. Kwame alone would remain of the Masters of Shadow, acting as a liaison between the dragons and the human-dominated world around them, although he would be stripped of his power through carrying out the ritual.

Halyfax, with Intari's aid, had disseminated an alternate plan to a precious few among their number that had ultimately voiced dissent against Kwame's ritual. Intari had made contact with Khesta Ogreson, a low orichite queen in the heart of the European subcontinent, who numbered among her children a chronomancer of some repute. The chronomancer, Enrid by name, helped them in secret, weaving a spell within their own parts of the ritual that would bend time itself to their will.

The ritual, which required the participation of each of the Masters of Shadow, would not go according to plan. Rather than draining all of the orichites of their essence to suffuse the dragons with their magical lore, the ritual would instead redirect the life force of Intari, Rakk, Yakra, and Halyfax into the empty husks of four other dragons. The chosen drakes had been dead from a time long before even Intari's birth, but known to Enrid, himself part of an order called the Masters of Time. The altered ritual would result in Zzethromandus' kin being thrust into a magical slumber, while the four chosen Masters of Shadow would wait, for as long as they must, in their own draconic forms.

By some method known only to him, Enrid agreed to project himself forward in time, asserting that his mastery over a strange school of mancy – what he called chaos magic – would aid them in their quest. The chronomancer corroborated the shadow dragons' prophecy of the events to come, having peered into the future himself. Blue orichalcum would indeed fade, and the Orichite Age would end, but both element and race would resurface, in terms that only Enrid seemed to understand.

He was a bit wild for Halyfax's tastes, but she believed in the low auric's skill, having heard of a pair of prisoners that recently appeared in his care, plucked from a different time that she knew nothing about. She was confident that the Masters of Shadow would be reawakened in their draconic forms, if not by the hands of Enrid himself, then by the hands of his progeny.

The chronomancer had insisted, much to Halyfax's chagrin, that he could only transport himself through time, and for an uncertain distance, given the volatile nature of the magic that he would use. Enrid was guarded about when, and where, he would appear in the future, and while Halyfax surmised that he himself may not have been certain, the chronomancer assured her and the others that he would be able to restore their draconic forms with his chaos magic.

The amount of time that it would take for Enrid, or those that came after him, to return the Masters of Shadow to life mattered little, Halyfax decided. As long as her magic and essence were intact, she could wait an eternity.

Halyfax and the three other chosen dared not speak of their plan to the rest of the Masters of Shadow, knowing that the dragon-sensitive Kwame at least would vehemently protest what he would perceive to be a perverse act. The others were better off not knowing what would occur, given that their protracted conversations had already taken a century to come to fruition. Even Intari, Rakk, and Yakra voiced their concern, not fully certain that they could trust Enrid's magic but unwilling to consign themselves to oblivion.

They would thank her later, Halyfax knew.

EPILOGUE

Late one evening, I received an urgent summons from the queen, requesting my immediate presence in Aurichome.

With not a few grumbles, Alina, Buster, and I left the Pitcher's little apartment in the Richmond that I had moved into, speeding along the light upper layer of traffic over the Golden Gate Bridge to arrive in the royal audience chamber around midnight.

We bustled into the room in a rush, racing past the AR artwork of Aurichome at war and up the carpeted stone steps to the queen's recessed pavilion. Tribe, Vasshka, Belinda, and Kwame, who all now lived in Aurichome, greeted us at the top of the stairs, having been waiting on our presence.

"What's the sitch?" Alina asked as we reached the dais.

The queen, alone except for our little group, was peering at her personal AR display, which currently portrayed a holographic image of Gloric, sandaled and seated on a pillow in his Reno sanctuary.

Fazgha graced us with a nod before returning her attention to the hologram. "The Sigil bears news that we dare not share over any network but his."

I started, wondering if there was intel regarding the ongoing investigation into Karthax's candidacy as mayor, or another plot by the Unaligned afoot.

"Celine's been helping me to look into the time stream to see if we can make contact with the future that the Nightpath visited," Gloric explained, indicating the young chronomancer at his side, who offered us a cheery wave from the Sigil's sanctuary. Her giant brother, the auromancer Andrew, sat nearby them, tinkering with an obsolete instrument that looked like a portable piano keyboard strapped to his chest.

"And?" I asked with interest.

Gloric shook his head curtly, his overlarge glasses and secondary lens display looking like goggles in the hologram. "Nothing. There's not even the hint of a line. It must have closed on your return."

I felt a pang of dismay, genuinely curious about the possibility of communicating through time as Gloric and I had when I was in the future.

"But," the Sigil continued, "with Celine's help, I have identified two signals in the past that bear considering."

"What? How?"

"There must be another chronomancer," the queen explained, "similar to our young friend, who has opened a channel on the other side of time."

I rocked back on my heels, not having considered that there could be another chronomancer out in time somewhere. I glanced at Kwame, who had a guarded expression on his face.

"Who do the signals belong to?" Alina asked.

All eyes in the room were on me and the Pitcher, the two of us being the only ones who had not yet heard Gloric's report.

"The first, we're unsure of," Gloric said slowly, his voice buzzing through the hologram.

I squinted, seeing the queen stiffen, and knowing before the gnome spoke the words to whom the other signal belonged.

"The second," Gloric said, his piping voice belying his excitement, "is unquestionably King Thog'run."

ABOUT THE AUTHOR

M. S. Farzan was born in London and grew up in the San Francisco Bay Area. He has written and worked for high-profile video game companies and editorial websites such as Electronic Arts, Perfect World Entertainment, Modus Games, and MMORPG.com, and has served as the Community Manager for games like *Dungeons & Dragons Neverwinter* and *Mass Effect: Andromeda.* He has trained in and taught Japanese martial arts for over fifteen years and has a Ph.D. in Cultural and Historical Studies of Religions.